Bluebeard and the Outlaw

Bluebeard and the Outlaw
A RETELLING OF BLUEBEARD/ROBIN HOOD

TARA GRAYCE

Bluebeard and the Outlaw

Copyright © 2021 by Tara Grayce

Taragrayce.com

Published by Sword & Cross Publishing

Grand Rapids, MI

Sword & Cross Publishing and the Sword & Cross Publishing logo are trademarks. Absence of ™ in connection with Sword & Cross Publishing does not indicate an absence of trademark protection of those marks.

Cover by MoorBooks Design

Moorbooksdesign.com

All rights reserved. Except for brief quotations in written reviews, no part of this publication may be reproduced, stored in a retrieval system, or transmitted in any form or by any means—electronic, mechanical, photocopying, recording, or otherwise—without prior written permission of the author.

This book is a work of fiction. All characters, events, and settings are the product of the author's over-active imagination. Any resemblance to any person, living or dead, events, or settings is purely coincidental or used fictitiously.

To God, my King and Father. Soli Deo Gloria

LCCN: 2021908673

ISBN: 978-1-943442-29-4

For the entire A Villain's Ever After gang: Camille Peters, Lichelle Slater, Nina Clare, Allison Tebo, Lea Doué, Alesha Adamson, W.R. Gingell, Lucy Tempest, J.M. Stengl, A.G. Marshall, and Sylvia Mercedes. I could not have asked for a better group of authors with whom to release a group series!

A special thanks to Camille, Lucy, and Allison for volunteering their names for Bluebeard's victims. You know you are a part of a great group of authors when you ask "Who wants to be brutally murdered?" and you get more volunteers than needed.

Chapter One

Perhaps you have heard the tale of the blue-bearded man and his murdered wives. Maybe you've wondered how a girl could be so foolish as to marry him. She must have been forced, you say. Or incredibly desperate.

Well, dear reader, I married him. But the legends don't tell the whole story. I might have been a fool. But I was the most reckless kind of fool, who believes she is a daring hero with legends of her own to make.

I raced through the trees, my cloak whipping behind me while I gripped my strung bow in my hand. My quiver bumped gently against my hip and leg with each stride. Only the pins I'd tucked through the fabric of the hood kept it firmly in place over my hair, hiding my long golden braid. The few strands that straggled free were short enough to appear to belong to a man, matching the fake mustache glued to my upper lip.

I had to suppress my wild laugh at the chase, my blood

thrilling as it pounded in my ears. Danger had such a sweet taste to it, formed as it was by a pinch of sour fear, a handful of bold passion, and a tang of near-death experiences.

Ahead of me, two of my merry band of brothers—Alan and Munch—hauled an iron-wrought chest between them. Behind me, Duke Guy of Gysborn and his men crashed through the undergrowth as they chased us.

Alan muttered between panting breaths, "Did you have to fill the chest with rocks?"

"It wouldn't look convincing otherwise." I glanced over my shoulder toward where Duke Guy, his sheriff, and his men blundered through the knee-high ferns and saplings. I motioned to my brothers. "Keep going. I'll slow them down and meet you at the hideout."

Neither Munch nor Alan wasted breath to argue with me.

I skidded to a halt next to a huge, sprawling live oak, then swung onto a low hanging branch. I settled into a comfortable standing position with my feet braced on two different, wide tree limbs. Gripping my strung bow in one hand, I tossed back the covering of my quiver that protected the delicate fletching and kept the arrows in place during more acrobatic maneuvers.

The duke and his men raced into sight as flashes of movement in the undergrowth, accompanied by the crunching of leaves, cracking of sticks, and the shouting of orders.

I selected an arrow from the remaining twenty-one left in the quiver. I had already used three arrows during the fake attack on the tax wagon. If all went well, my other four brothers—Will, John, Tuck, and Marion—would be executing the real attack on the tax wagon now that Alan, Munch, and I had led Duke Guy, Sheriff Reinhault, and the bulk of their soldiers away from their valuable cargo.

Duke Guy raced into view at the head of the pack of men. His black hair was cropped short while his beard was thick yet not long, and so black that flashes of blue appeared when sunlight glinted on the strands. Local gossip said that Duke Guy wore that beard to cover the scar his first wife had given him while he murdered her.

Considering Duke Guy had murdered three wives, it was entirely plausible that one of them had managed to scar him trying to defend herself.

Another injustice to add to Duke Guy's account, beyond his cruel taxation of the villagers during this prolonged drought. Three dead wives, and yet the king let him remain in charge of his dukedom. Claimed all three women killed themselves.

I didn't believe that for a second.

No matter the reason for his thick beard, it had given rise to the duke's nickname among the villagers, spoken whenever the duke, the sheriff, or their toadies were unlikely to overhear.

Bluebeard. A perfectly piratical nickname for a murderous duke.

Sheriff Reinhault sprinted at Duke Guy's heels. His blond hair was long enough to tie back while his face was angular and clean-shaven. The sheriff was Duke Guy's ever-faithful minion, collecting the high taxes from the villagers with alacrity and helpfully covering up any whiff of wrongdoing in the deaths of the duke's three wives.

I drew back the arrow, let out part of my breath and held the rest to steady myself, and released.

Almost too fast, Sheriff Reinhault grabbed Duke Guy and threw both of them behind the trunk of a large tree. My arrow passed harmlessly through empty air before thunking into a nearby tree.

Blast. Sheriff Reinhault had the reflexes of a hunted cockatrice.

The soldiers skidded to a halt, then went to ground

behind trees and thick stands of brush. They peeked around the trunks, hands on swords or reaching for their own hip quivers.

With all eyes fixed on me, I swept into a bow and deepened my voice. Another one of those reckless laughs bloomed in my chest and laced through my words. "Always a pleasure doing business with you, Duke Bluebeard."

Duke Guy pushed away from the tree, shaking himself free of his sheriff minion. He glared, his mouth a thin line surrounded by his blue-black beard. "You won't get away with this, Hood."

"I already have." I flourished another bow. As I straightened, I came up with an arrow already nocked. In one smooth motion, I released, my hands already in motion even as my first arrow sped through the air. I had three more arrows on their way within seconds.

Duke Guy dove for cover once again, his men following his example.

I leapt from my perch, landing lightly on my feet, before I took off running again. I dodged between the trees, leaping over fallen trunks. This forest was my home. My forester parents had walked with me down every path and hollow.

Even the ones that weren't entirely from this world.

Ahead, the faerie circle came into view. It was one of many in the Greenwood, though this was one of the largest. It was formed of a ring of spruce trees with a single arched opening leading into the bright clearing beyond.

At the entrance, the heavy, rock-filled tax chest had been abandoned. No other sign of my brothers remained.

Good. They had followed their orders and walked the faerie path ahead of me.

At the entrance, I glanced back at Duke Guy. His dark, burning eyes focused on me, his mouth twisting from its hard line into something born of fury. He halted, held my gaze as he raised his bow, and drew back the nocked arrow.

With my hood up, all he could see was the tall, cloaked figure known as the Hood. My fake mustache tugged painfully at my skin as I smirked at Duke Guy. I saluted him with my bow, dropped my free hand down to the iron rod stuffed into my quiver next to my arrows, then stepped into the faerie circle.

The magic of the faerie circle closed around me, heavy with an overwhelming floral scent. The world outside of the circle turned shimmering and hazy, like the waves of heat on a hot afternoon.

It was a place few would dare tread. A dangerous place for humans, unless they wanted to find themselves as some fae's plaything.

Behind me opened a doorway to another forest. This one was bathed in a sunlight far too bright. Everything was glaringly green and draped in vines and flowers. The otherworldly tugged with the thrill of utter adventure, luring me to step through that doorway into the Fae Realm.

If not for my brothers and the desperate villagers I'd leave behind, I would take that step. I would explore that far forest with all its thrills and dangers.

With the last of my willpower, I tightened my grip on the iron rod in my quiver. It kept the magic from disorientating me and reminded me of my mission.

No matter the lure, I couldn't leave. I had the villagers who saw me as their hero. The murderous duke and his sheriff lackey who provided me with all the adventure I could want. The duty of forester that my parents had left to me when they had died ten years before.

I drew in as deep a breath as I could manage of the heavy, fae air. If I stepped out of the circle at the wrong place, I would end up in a different part of the kingdom, perhaps even on the other side of the world entirely.

For that was how the faerie paths and their circles worked. They were the places where the Fae Realm touched the human world. While the circles in my forest only connected to that one faerie wood, that fae forest connected to many forests all across the human world. Or so my parents had always told me, as their parents and their parents' parents had told them. It was the knowledge that generations of foresters had gathered as they guarded this forest from the fae and fae monsters that could step through those circles.

I turned just a fraction before I stepped through the faerie circle back into the human world. Instead of spruce trees, I now stood outside of a perfect ring of maple trees with a circle of mushrooms growing at their base, a spot that was far deeper in the Greenwood than I had been moments earlier.

The angle of the sunlight through the autumn leaves showed that several hours had passed, even though I had been in the faerie circle for only a few seconds.

Duke Guy wouldn't dare to follow me into the faerie circle. The best he could do was put a watch on the circle, which would be in vain since I hadn't come out of the same circle where I had gone in. By now, he would be cursing the Hood, frustrated at his inability to capture the elusive outlaw.

Grinning to myself, I took the time to unstring my bow, secure it in its sheath underneath my cloak, and place the covering over my quiver once again. As I strolled through the forest, I carefully peeled off my fake mustache, wrapped it in a soft piece of cloth, then placed it in a small leather pocket set in the side of my quiver where it would be safe until the next time I reprised my role as the infamous Hood.

BLUEBEARD AND THE OUTLAW

I let myself whistle a tune as I walked, though I kept the volume low so that it wouldn't carry far in case Duke Guy had set his men to combing the forest, as they did periodically.

After fifteen minutes of hiking, I reached the secluded spot that served as our current hideout. It was tucked against a large boulder on one side with a fallen, uprooted tree providing further protection.

I waved at Marion as I passed where he was perched high in a tree, taking his shift as lookout.

He grinned and waved back with all the exuberance of his twenty years. He was slim and still so fresh-faced that my fake mustache gave me more facial hair than he had.

When I stepped into the hideout, Will was sharpening his sword while John and Alan sparred with wooden quarterstaffs. Tuck—short for Tucker—stopped stirring the pot of venison stew with his ever-present ladle. With his free hand, he fended off Munch, my youngest brother.

Munch's full name was Mungoe, much to his horror. My parents had progressively gotten more creative with their names, perhaps due to having six sons after their one daughter. Will and John had names so common that they shared their names with a dozen of the villagers. Alan's and Tucker's names were not quite so common, but not exactly rare either. Marion was still a respectable name, if unique. By the time they had gotten down to their youngest son, they had resorted to the moniker Mungoe from a story my mother had heard from a traveling bard.

And then there was me. Robin. The oldest of the bunch and the only girl. Perhaps my parents shouldn't have used up what was generally considered a boy's name for their daughter, even if they hadn't known I would be their only one.

But my mother had always loved the robins, waiting for

7

their arrival every spring with an anticipation that rivaled that of any holiday. For that, she had named me Robin.

It fit me. What else would be proper for a girl who stood six foot tall with calloused hands and hardened muscles? To be fair, my parents couldn't have known that, much less that I would spend the bulk of the last seven years masquerading as an outlaw.

I flourished my hands as my brothers all turned toward me. "Yes, yes. I know. The conquering hero has returned."

Munch rolled his eyes. "Only you call yourself that."

"Well, and the villagers. They call her that, and more." Alan shrugged as he dropped his quarterstaff. "They all but worship their outlaw."

"Which of course goes straight to her head." Will set aside his sword, pushed to his feet, and faced me. "I was beginning to get worried."

"Nothing to worry about. You know I can handle myself." I sauntered across the clearing and snagged the ladle out of Tuck's hand, deftly dodging his snatching hand as he tried to retrieve it. I sipped at the savory broth and managed to burn my tongue. Not that I let a hint of that show on my face as I smirked. "Delicious as always, Tuck. I'm famished."

Tuck yanked the ladle from my grip, grimacing at it. He wiped the ladle off on his apron before he stuck it back in the pot. "Rob, you're a menace."

"I'm sure Duke Guy is saying the same thing, and probably a few things that are much worse." I slouched onto one of the logs set around the fire and propped one booted foot on another log.

Will took the log next to the one I was using as a footstool. "The town is filled with happy people."

"At least until the sheriff comes around to collect taxes again." I rested an elbow on my knee. I'd ordered Will to don his own Hood disguise and take the money directly to the village before Duke Guy could get organized to go after them. The duke would certainly be puzzled, wondering how the Hood had managed to get from that faerie circle back to the village so quickly.

It just lent yet another tale to that inhuman mystique I was building for the Hood.

While I was the one who wore the role of the Hood most often, my brothers Will and Alan also took turns as the need arose, since they were the closest in hair color and build to me. After all, the man—or woman—beneath the cloak and hood didn't matter. It was all about the air of mystery, the whiff of legend.

Will picked up a stick and jabbed at the fire so forcefully that his stick snapped in his hand. "I wasn't kidding earlier, Robin. You need to stop taking such chances all the time. We're all in this together, you know. Alan and I already wear the hood. Even Marion and Munch could take turns soon. This doesn't have to rest entirely on your shoulders anymore."

I knew that. Of course, I did. I couldn't do this without any of them. Will was my stick-in-the-mud voice of reason that held back my most reckless impulses. John was the silent brawn, though when he spoke, I knew to listen. Tuck provided the food that kept us all going, as well as always being there when I needed him. Alan was my co-conspirator when it came to theatrics while Marion was the best of us when it came to sewing and mending, though Mother had made sure all of us knew such a vital skill. And, Munch could always be counted on to make me smile.

They were my merry band of brothers. More precious to me than any grand schemes of robbing Duke Guy and saving the villagers from excessive taxation.

With each robbery we pulled off, Duke Guy stepped up his security. He now had soldiers given to him by the king, and more would be on their way as soon as the king received word of this latest heist.

How long would it be before one of my brothers was hurt or killed in one of my dangerous schemes? I might thrive off the reckless thrills, but I couldn't ask my brothers to follow me into those adventures forever.

But until Duke Guy stopped taxing the villagers to death, I didn't have a choice. Still, I never made a lasting difference, stealing the money only to have Duke Guy tax it back shortly afterwards. It was a never-ending cycle.

How could I actually fix things? Besides killing Duke Guy, and he was proving to be difficult prey.

I shook my head and picked up my own stick, rolling it between my fingers. Ever since our parents had been found murdered outside of one of the faerie circles—by whom or what, we still didn't know and likely never would—I had been responsible for this family. It was a burden I couldn't seem to shake, even now.

Not that I would tell Will that. I gave him a grin and tossed the stick in the fire. "But where would the fun be in that? I rather like my hood, thank you very much. I'm not ready to give it up, even to you."

"The stew is ready!"

At Tuck's call, Will pushed to his feet. As he stepped over my leg blocking his way—I wasn't going to move it for him, of course—he nudged my shoulder. "Just think about it, all right? We can't keep doing this forever, you know."

I couldn't let him see how close his words were to my own thoughts just now. I was the arrogant outlaw called the Hood. Outlaws didn't have time for piddly things like doubts and worries.

Munch and Marion both stampeded to grab their bowls and shove their way into first place in line. Both of them stepped aside when John gave them a look and strode past them. At six foot nine, stocky, and bulky with muscles, John was by far the most intimidating of my brothers. Even I wouldn't dare step between John and food.

After a few minutes of scrambling around the stew pot, complete with Tuck's judicious use of his ladle, Alan broke away from the tumult carrying two bowls.

He handed one to me before he took a seat on Will's vacated log. "Rumor in town has it that the duke is angling to get married again and kill off yet another bride."

I stirred my stew, resting the bowl on my raised knee. "Let me guess, if the poor girl is breathing, has all her teeth, and is younger than forty, the duke will take her."

Considering his last three wives had died under mysterious circumstances—which everyone knew was murder, even if the law couldn't seem to find a reason to arrest him—he probably didn't care all that much about what wife number four looked like when he murdered her.

"Basically." Alan shrugged and spoke between spoonfuls of stew. "Perhaps some girl in the village will be desperate enough to risk her life in the hope of a few days of good food and access to the duke's riches."

The duke's riches…now there was a thought.

My hand stilled, my stew no longer my primary concern. Perhaps it was Will's nagging that spurred me to such a scheme. Maybe it was my own recklessness. But the plan unfolding inside my head would be the ultimate heist.

I set aside my bowl, then hopped lightly onto the tallest of our log seats. "Hold up, everyone."

John froze with his spoon partway to his mouth. Tuck halted with his ladle poised over the bowl he was filling.

I pointed to Alan. "Did the rest of you hear the rumor that the duke is looking for a wife?"

"He's doing what?" Munch's mouth hung open.

"Looking for a wife. Noising it about town as if he were

searching for a lost dog." Alan waved his hand. "Pathetic, really. What girl would be crazy enough to take him up on the deal, knowing he will likely kill her?"

"Actually…" I straightened my shoulders, my chest already filling with the anticipation of this next adventure. "I am."

Chapter Two

Yes, I know. It was a foolhardy plan to tie myself to a man known for killing his wives.

Oh, but it was a tempting, daredevil of a plan. And I wanted it with everything in me. A man might steal into a castle at night, dodging guards and making off with what he could carry. That was the stuff of legends, after all.

But I was a woman, for all I wore the disguise of a man. I could steal everything the duke owned in broad daylight by merely saying the two little words, "I do."

At my announcement, John dropped his bowl. Will's brow furrowed under the force of his glower. Marion started coughing on a bite of stew. Munch gaped while Alan just about fell off his log seat.

Tuck waved his ladle. "You can't be serious."

"Very serious." I gestured around our little hideout. "We can keep doing what we're doing, but it's never going to end. We steal the tax money and give it back to the people, only to have the sheriff take back that same money the next day. But if I marry the duke, I will have access to all his riches. We can rob him blind."

"Assuming he doesn't kill you on your wedding night." John scowled.

"Even better if he tries. Then I can be his widow and legally inherit everything. His riches, that fancy castle, all of it." I couldn't help but smirk at the thought. A long time ago, some duke more humane than the one ruling now had ensured that his particular dukedom could pass to daughters and even widows, even if it still was inherited by sons first of all. "If we pull this off, we'll finally be able to save the village from poverty and never have to steal again."

"You'd still have to marry the duke." Will scowled and glared. Only a year younger than me, Will had always been my right-hand brother. "It isn't safe. You could be hurt."

"As if dropping from trees, robbing tax wagons, and attacking royal guards is safe. I could just as easily be killed that way." I rolled my eyes. Safe wasn't something any of us had been in a long time. Not since our parents had been murdered in this very forest.

Alan shrugged and flourished a hand at me. "Give it up, Will. Have we ever talked Robin out of a plan when she sets her mind on something?"

"No, but...but this is..." Will huffed out a breath and jabbed a finger in my direction. "You can't seriously agree with the whole idea of her marrying the duke. He could hurt her."

A tense silence settled over the clearing. The rest of my brothers glanced from me to Will and back.

Then Alan broke into chuckles, hunching over to rest his hands on his knees from the force of his laughter.

Tuck joined him next, followed by John. Marion and Munch gaped as if they had all lost their acorns.

"You're worried for *Robin*?" Alan could barely pant the words between his laughter. "You realize what she'll do to the duke if he tries to lay a finger on her?"

Will's shoulders relaxed, and his mouth quirked into a smile at one corner. "Duke Guy doesn't stand a chance, does he?"

"Nope." I grinned and rested a hand on my quiver. What a lark this would be! I could beard the duke in his den, and he would never suspect a thing. I jumped down from the log and took my seat once again. "Listen up. Here's how we pull this off."

Tuck left the stewpot and his ladle to join the circle around the fire. The others set aside half-finished bowls of stew and leaned closer.

"First of all, we'll have to convince him I'm a traveling noblewoman." I rested my elbows on my knees. "Marion, do we still have that trunk of fancy dresses we took off that baroness a while back?"

Marion nodded and jabbed a finger toward the west. "It is still stashed in our storage cave deeper in the Greenwood. The dresses proved to be a hard sell here in the village."

"Good. I'll need several of them lengthened." I tapped my chin as I thought through all the facets of my disguise. "Alan, you'll pose as my elderly father. I'll be your youngest daughter whom you are desperate to marry off."

Still sitting, Alan hunched over and mimed leaning on a cane. "So dreadful to have an unmarried daughter of twenty-four still living under my roof. But she is such a comfort in my old age, you see. I would hate to part with her."

I raised my eyebrows at him. "Twenty-four?"

He gave a theatrical shrug. "You can pass for it, and you'll sound more marriageable to the duke if we claim you are twenty-four instead of twenty-nine."

He had a point, and I wasn't offended. Twenty-four was

old enough that an elderly noble father would be worried about having a spinster daughter still at home, but young enough to be appealing to a nobleman still in need of an heir. More appealing than my real age of twenty-nine, anyways. Yet, it was not so young that the duke, being in his low thirties, would think me too young for him.

Not that a man set on killing his wives likely cared. Perhaps he liked them young before he murdered them.

"Very well. Will and Munch, you'll come along as our guards." I waited until they nodded before I turned to the rest of my brothers. "John, you're too distinctive, and I would rather have you out here in case the duke does realize we aren't who we say we are. Tuck, you'll stay with him."

"What about me?" Marion all but bounced on his log seat.

I leaned even farther forward, lowering my voice. "I have a very special job for you, but you aren't going to like it."

"What is it? Why won't I like it?" Marion's mouth twisted between eagerness and suspicion.

He had good right to be suspicious, but I doubted he would realize what I had in store for him. "You're going to have to wear a dress."

"What?!" Marion reared back so fast he nearly tumbled from his log.

"I'm posing as a noble lady, and no lady travels without a maid, even if she is in the company of her father." I pressed my mouth into a line, trying to hide my smirk. "As you are the only one without so much as peach fuzz yet, it has to be you."

Even though Munch was a year younger than Marion, he already had more of a shadow of facial hair than Marion did. Something that Munch loved to rub in at every opportunity.

"But...but..." Marion glanced around at the others. Of course, they were all grinning with the sheer delight of this development. After a moment, Marion sighed and slumped. "Fine. I'll be the maid. But I won't like it."

I gave him a solemn nod, still working to hide the chuckles building in my chest. "Your protest has been noted."

Munch punched Marion's shoulder. "*Maid* Marion."

"Leave off." Marion punched him right back, harder.

"Don't tease him, Munch." I waggled my finger at him. "You don't have much for bristles yet either. I could still change my mind and make you the maid instead."

That snapped Munch's mouth shut in a hurry.

Will cleared his throat. "How will we explain our lack of horses or finery? Do you propose we steal everything we need to pull this off? We can't guarantee another noble party will travel through the Greenwood in the near future."

"We claim we were robbed by the outlaws of the Greenwood." I rolled my shoulders in a shrug. "The duke will be so furious at yet another outlaw attack that he won't question our story beyond that. And we know enough of our own methods to come up with a believable story of how we would have robbed a party like ours. We'll have only the one trunk, stuffed with women's things, to hide my weapons at the bottom."

Will nodded, his eyes glinting as if he was starting to see how this plan could actually work. "Won't the duke know the other noblemen of the court? He has been to the king's court occasionally."

That was a harder one to answer. I opened my mouth, but nothing came to me immediately.

"The lord of Loxsley is elderly." Alan flourished his hand as if he still held an invisible cane. "I doubt he would have traveled to the king's court often in the last number of years. He's a very minor lord, not one that a duke would associate with even if they were visiting the king at the same time. It would also explain any level of shabbiness in our appearance and roughness to our speech."

"Perfect. Thank you, Alan." I should have realized that Alan's nose for gossip would come in handy yet again. Loxsley was even in the right direction so that the duke wouldn't question that the lord of Loxsley would pass through the Greenwood on the way home from visiting the king's court. "Once I'm married to the duke, Will and Alan will continue on their way as if resuming their trip to Loxsley. The duke might offer horses or an escort, so you'll have to go along with them until you're off the duke's lands. Munch and Marion, you'll remain with me as my personal guard and maid."

I shot a glance at Will, telling him with my look that, see, I wasn't going to be entirely alone in the duke's lair.

Will gave me a sharp look right back. As if to argue that my two youngest brothers wouldn't be a lot of help if I got into real trouble. "How do you propose to signal us if you need aid?"

It was a good question. I might like to plan grand schemes for the best-case scenario, but Will was forever reminding me that I needed to plan for the worst as well. "I'll tie a white cloth in the window of whatever room I'm given. I'll put it up every morning, and take it down every night. If it goes up or comes down at any times other than dawn and nightfall, then you'll know I'm in trouble."

A white cloth in a window would stand out enough to be seen even at night. Besides, this system didn't have to work for long. Either Duke Guy would try to kill me within a few weeks and I would kill him, or I would find his piles of treasure and figure out a way to steal it.

All of my brothers nodded, but I turned to Munch and Marion. "I'm going to be counting on you to help me with the signal, especially you, Marion. As my maid, you'll have free access to my room in a way even Munch won't."

That seemed to mollify Marion a bit, knowing how crucial his role would be.

"Does anyone else have any questions?" I glanced around the circle of them. This would be our final, big score, and I could see that knowledge written on each of their faces. If we pulled this off, we would finally win the war we had been waging from the shadows for many years.

I probably should have been elated at that thought, but something in me quailed. I lived for the battle, the schemes, the thrills. What would I have left once it was over?

I couldn't dwell on that now. Right now, I was still the Hood. I was the daring outlaw quickly becoming a legend in my own time. I still had this one last heist to pull off, and it would be my most dangerous one yet.

Around the fire, all my brothers except for Will shook their heads that they had nothing else to add.

Will gave a shrug and a sigh. "I guess I have only one last question. When do you want to attempt this?"

Chapter Three

We were, of course, welcomed into the duke's castle. He even threw a grand dinner for us, as if fattening a pig before the slaughter. It didn't take much to have him demanding my hand right there over dinner, all while he shared dark, meaningful looks with his sheriff.

But I won't bore you with the details. Time is too short to waste for everyone but the fae.

I clasped Duke Guy's hands and faced him at the front of his grand hall. This was the closest I'd ever been to him, and this close I could see the line in his beard where the hair didn't lay quite right, giving credence to the rumor that there was a scar hidden underneath.

His eyes were a dark gray-brown, set deep above his large nose, a lump showing where it had once been broken.

But most impressive of all, I could meet his gaze without tipping my head down. If I hadn't been hunching to make myself appear shorter, he and I might have been the same height. He might even be a few inches taller.

It was a novel experience, looking a man in the eye so levelly. Besides my brothers, few men matched my height, much less surpassed me. Too bad he was a cruel, murderous duke. My heart might have been stirred otherwise.

The officiant took a deep breath and opened his mouth to launch into his speech.

Duke Guy gave a sigh, his fingers flexing on mine as if he was torn between gripping my hands tighter and letting them go. "Just skip to the end."

The officiant glanced at me, as if wondering what my thoughts were on that.

I shrugged, an action that rustled the pink velvet dress that was the fanciest of the ones Marion managed to lengthen on short notice. "Fine by me."

The officiant blinked at me for a moment before he cleared his throat and skipped ahead to the vows as instructed. It would be a shamefully quick wedding. But I was after a rather long con.

My heart was beating harder, and all I could think as I went through the marriage ceremony when prompted was *Say man and wife. Say man and wife.* Until the officiant said those words, Duke Guy would have a chance to realize something was wrong and back out.

I said *I do* at the right time, and so did he. When prompted, I simply stated my name as Robin. As much as it felt dangerous to use my real name, I couldn't risk this wedding being declared invalid because I had claimed anything else. If the duke found anything strange in me dropping my supposed title during our vows, his dark look never wavered.

In short order, the officiant stated in a deep voice, "I declare you man and wife. You may kiss the bride."

Right. I hadn't let myself think too much about that part. It felt wrong, to have my first kiss at the ripe old age of twenty-nine with this duke whom I more than likely would kill before the month was out.

Duke Guy released one of my hands to cup my chin. His callouses were rough against my skin, his fingers warm and large against my face. His eyes studied me for a moment before he leaned closer, whispering into my ear, "I know you hate me. I can see it in your eyes."

My mouth fell open as I sucked in a breath at his words. How much did he know? What did he suspect? And why had he married me anyway?

Before I had a chance to recover my wits, he planted a kiss on my mouth. Just the faintest peck that was so quick that I didn't even register the brush of his lips until his kiss was already over.

But as Duke Guy started to take a step back, turning away, my surprise morphed to anger. I wasn't the type to shrink under something as unsurprising as a kiss at a wedding.

No, this was the time to be bold.

I grabbed the front of the duke's shirt and pulled him close, my grip tight as if I intended to strangle him with a twist of his shirt's collar. As his eyes widened, I pressed my mouth to his. It wasn't much more of a kiss than he had given me. As I pulled back, I finally let my smirk break through my mask as I whispered, "You don't even know how much you hate me."

His eyes flicked over my face. I wasn't sure what he was searching for. Whatever it was, I didn't flinch under the scrutiny.

Perhaps I shouldn't antagonize him. But the danger of this banter was far more fun than keeping up the pretense of being a demure noble lady. Besides, he planned to kill me whether I was simpering or bold.

The officiant had said man and wife. At this point, it was either him or me. My life and his death, if I had my way.

After one last searing look, Duke Guy turned his cold gaze to the officiant. "You may go."

"Thank you, Your Grace." The officiant hustled out of there, casting glances back over his shoulder at me. Perhaps he was taking in one last sight of me, believing the next time he saw me would be when he was called to conduct my funeral.

Still holding my hand, Duke Guy turned us to face the few people who had witnessed our wedding. Sheriff Reinhault sat on a bench near the front while the duke's servants and guards had filled the benches behind him. Odd that they would be invited to something as prestigious as the duke's wedding.

Or, perhaps, not so odd. With this short notice, the duke had no one else to invite. Nor was his fourth marriage to a wife he planned to kill the kind of event to be marked with parties and feasting.

My brothers filled a single bench on one side. Will had his arms crossed as he scowled. Alan was regarding me with raised, bushy white eyebrows that completed his elderly disguise. Munch was openly gaping while Marion slouched in his bench with his legs sprawled apart in a very unladylike fashion, his mop-cap slightly askew. Even as I glanced at him, he adjusted the stuffings filling out the front of his dress.

I met his gaze and shook my head, and he dropped his hand. He made for a very unconvincing woman. If I didn't give myself away with my boldness, Marion's lack of acting skills would.

Duke Guy dropped my hand as if it was as clammy as dead fish, his eyes rather cold for a man who had just gotten married. "Say goodbye to your father. He will be leaving within the hour."

And so the game had begun. The duke had gotten what he wanted—a new, young bride to kill off at his leisure—so now he was moving to swiftly isolate me from my family.

This was his first move, but I had already made mine in marrying him. I had captured the castle and its duke. Now I just had to survive long enough to claim its treasure.

But there was something in his tone that grated on my instincts. I crossed my arms and faced my new husband. "Will his entire party be leaving?"

Duke Guy waved me off, already turning away from me toward his sheriff. "I am perfectly capable of providing a maid and a guard for my new wife."

As I suspected. He was systematically isolating me from everything and everyone. Apparently he had not just murdered his wives. He had killed them emotionally long before their physical death.

But he was going to find I was rather hard to kill.

I swaggered down the steps, my long strides hampered by the thick velvet catching around my ankles in a way that was unfamiliar after going around for so long in men's breeches instead of women's skirts. It seemed I was not convincingly womanly either.

I halted in front of my brothers. "Well, so far so good."

"Not so good." Will crossed his arms and glowered at me. "What was that? You *kissed* him."

Of course that was the part Will would get all steamed about. I smirked, crossing my arms right back. "Just keeping the game interesting."

"You didn't have to make it that interesting." Will muttered, his scowl deepening.

Will was *such* a stick-in-the-mud.

"It's about to get even more interesting." Alan shifted, thumping his cane as if he were still in character even as he spoke in his normal voice. "A guard just gave the order for us to leave. *All* of us. Even Munch and Marion."

"I know. Duke Bluebeard told me." I shrugged. "It doesn't change anything. It isn't like Marion was going to pass for a maid much longer." Even as I spoke, I swatted Marion's hand as he was reaching to adjust his fake bosom yet again. He was decidedly lopsided now, but poking at it was just making it worse.

"Of course it does." Will faced me, not backing down. "It's not too late. We can still make a break for it. You shouldn't stay here alone."

No way was I leaving now. Not when this scheme was turning out to be even more of a heady challenge than I had imagined. "I'll be fine. The plan doesn't change. We already have all the signals worked out. If anything, I'll feel better having even more of you on the outside in case I do need help, rather than have Munch and Marion caught in the same trouble with me."

"I still don't like it." Will grimaced, his fists clenched.

"This is my call." I held his gaze until, finally, he was the one who looked away. I drew myself straight, my back popping after I had been hunching so long to try to appear shorter. "You have your orders."

Will's jaw worked, but he nodded. Munch and Marion shifted, looking away uncomfortably. Alan gave me a nod and lifted his cane in a salute. "We have your back."

"I know." I would have reached out and clapped my brothers on the back but that wasn't the action of a daughter to my elderly father, guards, or handmaid.

Will's gaze focused on something past me, and his shoulders stiffened.

I turned to find Duke Guy striding across the room toward us at a brisk pace, his lackey Sheriff Reinhault dogging his heels. When the duke reached my side, he held out his arm, his expression impassive. "I will show you to your room, my lady."

I eyed his arm for a moment. As far as I remembered, the duke's previous wives weren't murdered on their wedding night. And he had said that he was bringing me to *my* room, not to *our* room. Maybe I was reading too much into his wording. Or, perhaps, he was wary enough not to want a woman who hated him too close to where he slept.

He had reason for wariness. I was no pawn in this game to be killed off on a whim.

As I took his arm, Duke Guy gestured from the sheriff to my brothers. "My sheriff will show you to the stables and provide an escort from the boundaries of Gysborn."

My poor brothers would have to spend the better part of a day circling back to the Greenwood after being escorted so far in the wrong direction. But they wouldn't dare break their cover with the sheriff's men.

It meant I would be essentially on my own, except for Tuck and John still waiting in the Greenwood.

That probably shouldn't give me a delicious thrill.

Duke Guy spun on his heel and headed for the door, taking me with him. I glanced over my shoulder at my brothers one last time. Even Alan's gaze remained solemn. Will still scowled. Munch and Marion gaped, as if they couldn't believe I was actually going through with this.

So many sober faces. As if this wasn't a grand adventure the likes of which I would never find again.

Just before Duke Guy pulled me from the room, I gave my brothers one slow, cocky wink.

As the large double doors slammed shut behind me, I faced forward again.

The long, dark corridor stretched before me, lit only by the rare, flickering candle in a sconce. A deep red carpet ran down the center, as if placed there to hide the blood that would likely be spilled in this place.

Beside me, Duke Guy remained silent and brooding, his gaze fixed ahead. He strode at a long, quick pace that someone shorter than I would have been trotting to match. As it was, I reveled in the pace. It was rare that I didn't have to shorten my stride for others.

He led me through the twisting hallways until we arrived outside of the room in the south tower that I had been given upon my arrival the night before.

With a lightning move, Duke Guy twisted from underneath my hand and planted his hands against the wall on either side of me, trapping me without ever touching me. He leaned closer, as if trying to intimidate me by looming over me.

I was too tall for any looming, and his action just brought his eyes level with mine, inches apart. We were well matched, he and I. And, oh, how that made this battle so much sweeter.

"What is your game, Lady Robin?" He spoke the words in a low growl. We were alone in this hall, his body large as he crowded me against the wall. This close, the candlelight played blue shadows across his hair and beard.

Bluebeard, indeed.

I tipped my head, letting a hint of my teasing grin play across my mouth. "And what game do you think I play?"

"It is said I killed my three previous wives, and yet here you stand quite willingly married to a monster." He was so close now that his hot breath mingled with mine in the space between us. "If you were smart, you would have run while you had the chance."

"Perhaps my game is as simple as power." I knew how to be daring as an outlaw, but now was the time to be daring as a woman. I walked my fingers up Duke Guy's chest, gratified when his dark gaze swung away from me for a moment in something almost like a flinch. "I am the youngest of my father's children. My brother and his wife will inherit my father's estate. My sister-in-law is the lady of the household. She has the power of producing and raising its heirs. If I want to claim that power for my own, I had to look elsewhere for an estate in need of a wife and an heir. Perhaps I think I can tame a monster."

I was treading dangerous territory, taunting him with the prospect of an heir that I had no intention of giving him.

But it was the only lie that would fit with both my brashness and my cover story.

"If that is the case, then you should kill me now and save both of us further heartache." His gaze swung back to mine, the muscle at the corner of his jaw twitching beneath his beard.

I smoothed my hand over his chest at the collar of his shirt. The knife I wore secured to my side and accessible through a pocket of my dress taunted me. It would be so easy to draw it now and plunge it into his stomach. I could end all of this right here and now.

I hesitated. I told myself that it was because I needed his death to appear to be self-defense, and it would appear suspicious to everyone if he died of a stabbing only minutes after the wedding. Sure, no one was around. No one could counter my statement if I claimed I stabbed him to defend myself.

But even as I lied to myself, I couldn't fully ignore that I didn't want this game to end so quickly. There was no thrill in stabbing him now. There had been no chase. No hard-fought battle. No close brush with death. No sting of fear on my tongue and wild beat of action in my veins.

It would be a wholly unsatisfactory victory for him to die before our game had truly begun.

So, instead, I traced my finger up his neck along the

artery that ran there, vulnerable beneath such a thin layer of skin. "It doesn't suit my purposes to kill you just yet."

For a moment, he stared down at me, his mouth pressed into a tight, grim line. His jaw remained hidden under that thick, blue-black beard. When he finally spoke, his tone cracked hard in his deep voice. "Then, when this is done, don't say I didn't warn you."

With that, he pushed away from the wall and stalked off down the corridor until his descent down the curving staircase hid him from view.

When he was out of sight, I entered my set of rooms. A lavish red carpet covered the floor from one dark-paneled wall to the other in both the front sitting room and the rear bedchamber. Cushioned chairs and a couch sat by the fireplace in the sitting room, providing a cozy place to retreat.

Inside the bedchamber, a massive four-poster bed filled the room. Light filled the space from the three narrow windows set next to each other with a window seat beneath. The thick, velvet curtains were also blood red and edged with gold tassels and trimmings.

My new husband certainly had a thing for that deep red color.

I crossed the room to where my trunk remained at the foot of the bed. I had expected to have Marion as my "maid," but now my new husband Duke Bluebeard would assign me a maid loyal to him. I would have to find a better hiding spot for my sword, bow, and quiver, which were currently hidden at the bottom of my trunk.

I took in the room, trying to figure out where a maid was unlikely to stumble across something I stashed. The wardrobe was obviously out. The cleaning maids would change the bed coverings frequently, so under the bed or the mattress was also out.

After another scan of the room, I strode to the window

seat. It was built into the ledge formed by the thickness of the castle wall. But the cushions were placed on a wooden box built over the stone.

After setting the cushions on the floor, I inspected the top of the window seat. Only a few nails held it down, and it sounded slightly hollow beneath, as if there might just be a few inches of space between the wood and the stone of the castle's wall.

It took a bit of effort, but I managed to pound and pry the wide oak board off, using my dagger. As I had hoped, a hollow space had been left underneath, boxed in by wooden boards along the edges to hold up the top. The space had most likely been left to prevent the board from rotting, as it would have if it had been laid directly over the damp, chill stones.

With the hilt of my dagger, I pounded the nails free from the top board where they wouldn't get in the way when I placed the board back over my new hiding place. I stashed the nails, my sword, bow, quiver, and Hood outfit in the hollow. It was a tight squeeze, but the board fitted over the space snugly enough that I doubted it would be found.

After that was done, I piled the cushions back in place. Returning to my trunk, I pulled out a long strip of white silk I had taken from one of the dresses we had cut up to add length to the dresses that fit me. Crawling on the window seat, I cranked the window open, its leaded glass panes heavy and solid. Once a crack opened at the top, I stood and tucked one end of the white cloth into the space. When I cranked the window closed again, it pinned the cloth into place.

That done, I sat on the window seat, stared out at the forest sprawling away from the castle, and plotted my next move.

Chapter Four

Was I playing with fire? Definitely. But I had no intention to stop until I had gotten just a little bit burned.

After taking a few minutes to plan, I left my room to wander—well, case—the castle in the time I had before the midday meal.

A guard was stationed outside my door, and he nodded to me as I exited my room. I ignored him as a proper lady would, though inside I was seething. The duke might claim that the guard outside my door was for my protection, but I knew the truth. That guard was there to keep an eye on me, something that was confirmed when he left his post to trail behind me.

I meandered through the maze of corridors and long galleries, complete with red carpet runner down the center, gold wall sconces, and rows of weapons hanging on the walls. Even if all I did was nick the sconces and the weapons, I could set up my merry band for a while.

I passed a few servants in the halls. Most glanced away as soon as they saw me and didn't seem inclined to interact. It could be because I was the lady or it could be the duke's watch dog trailing after me, ready to report every move the servants and I made.

Some of the servants were vaguely recognizable from the village. But I didn't know any of them. Not really. The villagers and the castle dwellers kept to their separate lives, only crossing occasionally.

Despite the duke's atrocities, the castle servants and soldiers had shown remarkable loyalty to him. Perhaps because their jobs depended on him even more than the villagers, who paid him rent and taxes for the land they worked but were otherwise left to make a living as they pleased.

Finally it was the time for the midday meal. I worked my way to the formal dining room and flung open the double doors.

Duke Guy already sat at the head of the long, oak table with Sheriff Reinhault at his right. A place had been set for me at the foot of the table.

Yes, it was the proper seat for the lady I was pretending to be. But, it was a ridiculous seating arrangement with only the three of us. I wasn't sure what I was going to do about it, though.

Duke Guy and Sheriff Reinhault pushed to their feet as I approached the foot of the table. Duke Guy graced me with a nod. "I trust your rest was refreshing."

His tone was so distantly polite, as if he was greeting a guest instead of his new wife, that it grated on my daring streak.

"Yes, it was. I was so desperately weary after the trial of marrying you this morning." I sauntered toward the table, not bothering to hide the bite in my voice.

BLUEBEARD AND THE OUTLAW

As I reached what was supposed to be my seat, a footman dashed from his place along the wall and pulled out my chair for me. I halted for a moment, just staring at the chair. I'd never had my chair pulled out for me before. It was an odd feeling, letting someone else do something that I was perfectly capable of doing for myself.

But it did move the chair enough to make what I had in mind easier to pull off in a dress.

In one swift motion, I gathered up the flatware and plate, hopped onto the chair, and from there onto the tabletop. Ignoring all the eyebrows raising at my action, I marched down the center of the table. My dress might not have been a royal cape, but there was something powerful in the swish of a velvet dress.

The footman, the duke, and the sheriff stood frozen, just gaping at me—or as much as the duke ever gaped.

When I reached the far end, I had to lift my skirt to step around the platters of venison, vegetables, and fruit already laid out. Of course, I wasn't going to step in them and waste perfectly good food.

I hooked the chair to the duke's left with my toes and dragged it out from under the table enough that I could hop down, then plop into it. While the duke still stared at me, I laid out the plate and flatware once again. I wasn't sure what all the forks and spoons were for, especially for something as simple as a midday meal, but the fancy folk here at the castle set store by such things.

Grabbing one of the forks by my plate, I speared a chunk of venison. "Don't halt your discussion on my account. I'm sure whatever the duke and his sheriff discuss over dinner is fascinating."

Duke Guy slid into his seat, casting a dark look at Sheriff Reinhault. If I didn't know better, I'd say there was some tension there. "We were just discussing the weather."

Sheriff Reinhault gave Duke Guy a sharp-edged smirk, before he turned a far more disarming smile on me. "I believe the weather is about to take a turn for the better. It feels like rain to me."

"Oh, really? The rain is desperately needed." I bit into the venison, eating it from the fork rather than putting it on my plate and cutting it properly. We often ate like that in the forest. Why wash plates when we could just eat right out of the pan?

Maybe I should keep up more of a pretense of proper behavior, but I was in the mood to tweak the duke just enough to get him annoyed, now that I was securely married to him.

Since the sheriff seemed more inclined to speak with me than the cold-eyed duke, I faced Sheriff Reinhault across the table. "How can you tell it's going to rain? Do you have an old wound that aches? A bum knee?"

"Just a feeling." Sheriff Reinhault sprawled back in his chair, a hint of a smile playing around his mouth. While the duke was all dark and brooding—dark eyes, black hair, glowering expression—Sheriff Reinhault was all sunny blond hair tied back, sky blue eyes, and easy smiles, as shown by the deep smile lines around his mouth and eyes.

"Hope it turns out to be more than just a feeling." I stuffed the rest of the venison in my mouth and studied the silent interplay between the sheriff and the duke. The duke was glaring at the sheriff, almost as if he didn't want the rain.

But, perhaps, he didn't. This was the infamous Duke Guy "Bluebeard." He enjoyed the subjugation of his people, and it was far easier to keep them in misery when they were barely scraping by as it was.

I claimed an apple and crunched into it, causing the duke to start.

Duke Guy set down his flatware and pushed away from

the table. "Reinhault, gather the men. I wish to search the faerie circles again this afternoon."

I refused to stiffen. The duke planned to search the forest for the Hood. Our hideout was well hidden and Alan, Will, Marion, and Munch would still be with the duke's men as they were escorted from the dukedom. But John and Tuck would be close to the castle, keeping an eye on me. I didn't like the thought of them facing Duke Guy without me there.

Besides, I hadn't gotten married to Duke Guy to get shunted off to the side. I had to spend time with him to mine his secrets.

I jumped to my feet and wrapped my hand around his arm. It was strange, holding the crook of his arm like this, feeling the strength of his well-muscled sword arm beneath my fingers. It was a strength he would wield against me, if he ever caught me as the Hood. "Aren't you going to give me a proper tour of the castle? We were married this morning, after all. I would like to see my new home."

A tour was something he should have done, rather than just dump me off at my room earlier in the day as if I was a piece of luggage.

His shoulders lifted in a sigh as he swung his gaze to the ceiling for a moment. "Reinhault, proceed without me. It seems I will be showing the castle to my new wife."

Sheriff Reinhault's smirk was back as he stood, bowed, and strode from the room.

When the sheriff was gone, Duke Guy rested his heavy gaze on me, not speaking, just staring.

I was not the type to give him a winsome smile, and there was no way I would ever manage innocent pleading. Instead, I set off, tugging him along before he fell into step with my quick pace.

Thankfully, the guard didn't follow us, and my shoulder blades stopped itching with that feeling of eyes upon me.

Duke Guy likely wouldn't show me his treasure vaults on this tour. But I would learn just as much by noting where he didn't show me. It would narrow down where in the castle I would have to search later.

Besides, the better I learned the castle here in the daylight, the easier it would be to navigate in the dark.

For long moments, we strode down one of the imposing, armor-lined galleries in an oppressive silence. As we reached the end of the gallery, Duke Guy opened his mouth, paused, then closed it again.

I supposed he wouldn't have much to say to the wife he was plotting to murder.

That meant it was up to me to carry the conversation.

As we stepped from one armor gallery to a portrait gallery, I gazed about as if in awe of the grandeur. It wasn't that much of a stretch. I was in awe—and trying to figure out what I could steal that could be quietly resold. "This is quite different from Loxsley."

"I suppose it is." Duke Guy's murmur was deep and rumbling inside his chest. "I have never had the pleasure of visiting."

Perfect. That would make my lies easier to maintain. I would still want to be vague, in case someone who really was from Loxsley happened to travel through before I carried out my heist.

"Perhaps we can visit someday soon. I do so miss my family." That was the expected thing to say, right?

Duke Guy raised an eyebrow at me. "I thought you were so desperate to leave your family home that you were willing to marry me."

Ah, right. The fictitious evil sister-in-law. I truly hoped none of my real sisters-in-law—if my brothers ever retired from thievery long enough to get married—didn't end up as stereotypically malicious as this fake sister-in-law of mine.

"Well, I do have to return home and rub this place in my sister-in-law's face. On second thought, perhaps I should invite my family to visit here first before we make any trips there."

"Hmm." It was a noncommittal sound with a hint of disapproval. As if he didn't like my attitude toward this non-existent relative.

He was one to judge. He had murdered three wives. A little fake rivalry on my part was hardly something to earn me that dark judgment in his gaze.

As we talked and walked, we passed doors to several rooms. The library. The study, of which I made particular note. It would be a good place to snoop through later.

At the end of the hall, we stepped into the base of one of the towers. The inside of this room had been plastered white, and magical creatures from the Fae Realm had been stuffed and mounted. Some were just heads, like the basilisk head hung between two of the windows, its marble eyes sightless and its mouth gaping open in a permanent hiss. Others were full body mounts that filled the space of the room, such as the mount of a chimera with its lion's head, goat body, and snake-headed tail.

I let go of the duke's arm to wander the room, reading the gold plaques set beneath the fae monsters. The plaques listed the name or names of those who had killed the fae beasts and the date. Some of these monsters had been killed by previous dukes while many of the others had been dispatched by Greenwood foresters. My ancestors.

I halted by a three-headed serpent. Its plaque confirmed what I had already known. My parents had been the one to take down this one.

I worked to control the rise of emotions. Those names wouldn't mean a thing to me if I really had been a lady from the far-off Loxsley.

Duke Guy halted next to me, his hands clasped behind me. "I suppose I shouldn't have brought you here. It is shocking to see the fae beasts up close."

Much less shocking when they were dead and safely stuffed. Here, I could simply admire their strength and ferocity captured here, with a faint hint of fae magic still clinging to them. They were far more thrillingly scary when facing them in person after they had crawled through a thin spot into the human world from the Fae Realm.

But in my role as a lady, I couldn't admit that I had faced beasts like these while they were still alive, though none of the beasts I had killed had made it into this room. I had just begun my training with my parents when they had been killed. And within a year after that, the duke's parents had died, he had assumed his title, he had disbanded the foresters, claiming them unnecessary, and the rising taxes and lack of a job had forced me into a life of outlawry.

I shook myself. While I had been looking at the mounted magical beasts, I had worked my way to the far side. Here, I could see the opening to the staircase that curved out of sight upward. Beside the staircase, a small wooden door set into the wall, almost as if it was trying to be overlooked.

Something about that door itched at my senses. The same way a fae beast did when it was lurking in the Greenwood.

I pointed to the staircase first. "What is up there?"

"My rooms." Duke Guy's voice deepened in a forbidding tone.

I might be his wife, but his rooms were apparently off limits even for me. Not a problem. I had no intention of being a real wife, and I would just sneak up there at some point when I was sure he wasn't there.

Trying to maintain my casual demeanor, I gestured to the small door. "And what's that?"

"Never open that door. Ever." He all but growled the

words, his tone so dark that I might have quailed if I'd had less of a spine. He gripped my arm firmly, though not hard. "Please. Do not open that door."

"I won't." I daintily set my hand on his arm again. "Why don't we continue the tour?"

The first chance I got, I was going to open that door. It most likely concealed the duke's greatest treasure, if he was this protective of it.

AFTER A QUICK DETOUR on my way to my room, I took down the white cloth at sunset and retired early. I caught a few hours of sleep before I forced myself to get up in the middle of the night. I dressed in the tunic, trousers, and cloak that I had smuggled into the castle with me. Something in me relaxed now that I was once again dressed as the Hood.

The guard outside my room posed a little bit of a challenge. I couldn't exit my door without him seeing, nor could I simply break into the connecting servant's room since that door was also in the guard's view.

That meant I would have to brave a climb down the castle wall on this nearly moonless night, a wonderfully perilous endeavor at best.

After stuffing my stockings inside my boots and tying the bootlaces together, I slung one boot over my shoulder and wiggled through the window. With my toes, I felt for a secure footing before I moved either of my hands from their grip on the window casing.

Inch by inch, I worked my way down from my window to the window of the room below. In the dark, the drop was disappointingly obscured, and the climb barely provided a thrill.

When I reached the window, I found it still cracked open

as I had left it when I had ducked into the room after my tour with the duke and before my guard located me once again. It was difficult pulling the window open, forcing the crank mechanism to turn. Once I had the opening wide enough, I wiggled inside, dropping onto the window seat.

After sneaking from the room—no guards in sight—I went straight to the storage room I found earlier in the day on the tour with the duke. I looped a coil of a long rope over my shoulder and carried it back to the room below mine. That rope would make it a lot quicker to nip out of my room to the forest to confer with my brothers if needed.

That done, I navigated through the castle until I reached the tower that contained the duke's rooms. Here, too, he had guards, but they were pacing in a rotation rather than stationed in one place. I slipped past them in the brief moment when their backs were turned at the far end.

Once inside, I crept between the monster mounts, their shapes forming grotesque, black silhouettes in the near darkness. The luring danger of that door drew me to it until I stood at the far end of the room.

For a moment, I hesitated between the twin tugs of danger. There was the danger of the mysterious door, a siren call of lurking menace.

Then there was the staircase to the duke's rooms. He was currently up there, sleeping soundly in the safety of his castle. It would be so satisfyingly thrilling to sneak up there and taunt him in the guise of the Hood.

But I couldn't kill him or wake him by putting a knife to his throat just yet. I still needed to locate his treasure trove.

Maybe I could leave a note. A very taunting note. Even better, I would be here to see him read it, playing the role of dutiful wife.

Perhaps on another night. For tonight, my goal was breaking into that small door.

I withdrew my lock pick set from a pocket and set to work. Lockpicking was more about feel and finesse than sight, so the lack of light didn't bother me. After inserting the pick, I felt around inside the lock, quickly finding the two pins.

This should be simple. A mere two pins.

Yet, when I added tension to the lock with a second pick, I couldn't seem to get the two pins to catch no matter how hard I tried.

I gritted my teeth and kept at it. This shouldn't be that hard. Sure, I wasn't as good at lock picking as Will. He had successfully picked intricate ten pin locks placed on the tax collection wagons. A two pin lock should have taken a mere minute or less.

After fifteen minutes of struggle, I was about ready to stab something with my lock pick. After half an hour with no success, I nearly gave in to the temptation to use language that my parents would have punished me for uttering.

After an hour, I stepped back and glared at the door. I should have been able to pick that lock. It was almost as if the lock didn't want to be picked. Or couldn't be picked.

I rested my hand on the door and closed my eyes. As I focused, I sensed the distant hum of fae magic that wasn't the lingering traces of magic on the dead fae beasts but instead came from the room beyond this door.

Whatever this was, it wasn't a treasure vault, unless the duke guarded his treasure with fae magic.

Which would mean *he* would have to possess magic of his own.

My parents had never mentioned that the dukes of Gysborn had descended from the fae. Surely if the duke's father or mother had been a fae, it would have been the talk of the village. And if he'd had a fae parent, his ears would show at least a hint of a taper.

Perhaps a grandparent? Or great-grandparent? It couldn't be much farther back, otherwise the trace of magic would be too small for the magic I was sensing behind that door.

My own magical senses came from a distant fae ancestor, though my parents had taught all of us to hone that sense through a lot of practice.

No matter how this magic got here, it meant that this had turned into more than a mere heist. I was still a forester's daughter, tasked with guarding the Greenwood and the local villages from incursions by the fae. If the duke was using fae magic as part of his harassment of the villagers, then it was my job as both a forester and the Hood to stop it.

Chapter Five

The fae. Faeries. The fair folk.

They go by many names. Come in many shapes and sizes. Like any people, some are sweet and gentle and good to each other and to humans.

But others are cruel and twisted.

Now that I was paying attention, I could sense the faint tingle of fae magic throughout the entire castle, so subtle and constant that it had been easy to overlook. There was fae work here, sure as darkness, and it wasn't the good kind.

But I was a forester. A hunter. The fae, like any prey, could be brought down as long as you had the right weapon.

I woke to an unfamiliar plinging. I lifted my head and just stared at the windows as rain pattered the glass, leaving behind fat drops that rolled down the pane before dripping onto the sill.

It was raining. Sheriff Reinhault's hunch had been correct.

After another moment, I threw off the covers and rushed to don the ugliest dress of the ones Marion had modified for me—a monstrosity in mauve with too many ruffles and a ratty ivory lace added to the hem to make it long enough for me. Over this, I pulled on a cloak that was even uglier, a vomit yellow-green as it was. But it was the only ladies' cloak we'd had back in our camp.

Hurrying past the guard, who fell into step behind me, I strode down the hallway, wound my way through the corridors until I reached the nearest tower, and climbed the stairs until I found the door to the wall top.

I tipped my face up as I stepped from the castle's interior into the pounding rain. The rain was cold, the breeze chilly, yet I strode farther onto the wall top. Clammy water ran down my neck and soaked the collar of my dress.

The guards patrolling the wall top gave me a wide berth, even as they cast me sideways glances. There was something heady about walking on the wall top of the duke's castle surrounded by his guards with complete impunity.

As I approached the center of the wall, I found another figure already leaning against the wall there, a figure wearing a black cloak and slightly taller than I was.

I marched to his side, my skirts increasingly damp and clammy in the rain. I leaned against the battlements next to him. "It seems Sheriff Reinhault was right about the rain."

"He always is." Duke Guy's voice rumbled from beneath his hood. He slumped against the stone, his head bent so that I couldn't see his face besides a bit of his beard. In the rain, the black beard was glossy, but lacking the blue sheen.

"It must be handy, to have a sheriff who can so predict the weather." I stared out over the forest to the north, the croplands in all directions. This rain was good and was desperately needed, but it was so heavy that it was more likely to run off the parched earth than soak in as a lighter rain would.

"He is rarely wrong." The duke's shoulders sagged further at that.

I shifted against the wall, trying to get a better angle to see his face. I had to spend time with him to learn where he kept his treasure and how best to steal it. But I had already had a tour of the castle—a very awkward, mostly silent tour. What else was there to do together? If the duke had been one of my brothers, I would have challenged him to a friendly bout with a sword or a quarterstaff. Or perhaps archery practice—well, contest.

A duel with the duke would be riotous good fun. Too bad it would break what little cover I had left.

Even as we stood there, the deluge gushed down even harder from the charcoal gray clouds hanging heavy and low. A gray sheet of rain obscured the trees of the Greenwood and the rooftops of the village.

Duke Guy straightened, pushing away from the wall. "You should go inside before you catch a chill."

"While you stay out here catching a chill?" I turned to him, my cloak fully soaked and providing little protection. Water streamed down my face, dripping off the end of my nose.

"The river will be rising. I need to evacuate the village." Duke Guy spun on his heel, striding away from me at a quick clip. Dismissing that I had anything to offer in this situation.

I huffed out a breath, spewing some of the flooding rain from my face. Even if I had been a true noble lady, I could have helped in the form of organizing dry clothes, blankets, and shelter for the evacuated villagers. One would think he hadn't been married three times for how little he valued a wife's contribution.

Not that he could be said to value his wives that highly since he had murdered them in the end.

I caught up with him just inside the door to the tower and grabbed his arm firmly enough to halt him in his tracks. For a moment we stood there, both of us dribbling streams of rainwater onto the stone floor. I met the duke's gaze and held it. "I am going to help."

Perhaps it was the iron in my tone and my gaze. Or maybe he was just too worried about flooding to argue.

He simply nodded, then set off at a swift pace down the stairs.

I hiked my heavy, sodden skirts and hurried after him, cursing that I couldn't change into my tunic and trousers. They would be much more practical, and the wool cloak for my Hood disguise would be much warmer than this fancy once I'd donned.

But I couldn't risk that someone would recognize the outfit. I would just have to make do with the dress. At least it was an ugly dress.

Duke Guy burst into the room at the base of the tower, where several guards gathered. He swept his sharp gaze at the soldiers, causing them to straighten and salute. The duke pointed at the nearest. "Go to the stables and see to readying horses for myself, my lady, and a squad of men." As that soldier ran out the door into the pouring rain, the duke jabbed at the next guard. "Tell the captain to ready a squad of men. And, you, see to fetching all the wagons we have on hand. We'll bring the village stores here so that they won't be ruined."

I stiffened. The villagers were not going to like that. Bad enough that the duke stole all their money in the form of taxes. They would riot if the duke swooped in and started loading up wagons with all the food they had scraped together. Food that would be desperately needed to get through the winter.

Yet the river ran through the middle of the village. In a normal year, even a normal flood year, the storehouses were built well above the flood line. But this rain, coming after years of drought, would cause a flood like nothing we had seen in a long time.

I was the last person who would advocate bringing the grain and dried foods to the duke's castle, but…this situation was dire.

The stricken villagers would hesitate to accept any help from the duke. They would be suspicious, and rightly so.

This was a mission for the Hood, even if I couldn't make an appearance as the infamous outlaw. It would be up to me to convince the villagers to seek shelter and safety the duke offered. An odd position to be in.

Duke Guy glanced to me, then he beckoned. "Come."

I crossed my arms and just stared right back. I wasn't one of his men to be ordered about in that curt tone.

He heaved a sigh and softened his expression and his beckoning motion. "Please. If you are going to help, you will need warmer clothes. We have the time. The horses and wagons will take a few minutes to ready."

He made sense, and now I was curious. It was almost as if he was taking a tiny thought of care for my wellbeing. I wanted to see what that flicker of care would look like.

Instead of striding ahead, Duke Guy kept pace with me, even as he led me through the hallways until we reached the room filled with mounted magical monsters. I glanced at the mysterious small door, even as the duke swept us past it and up the stairs leading to his room.

I probably should have hesitated. After all, the duke was leading me up to his room.

But, I could feel his tension and see his hurry in the swiftness of his steps that had even me with my long legs trotting to keep up. This was a man so focused on the mission that he had nothing else on his mind.

Besides, I was curious to see his room. I hadn't had a chance to case it yet, and it would make it much easier to sneak around in the dark if I had seen it in the daylight.

He ascended the stairs at a rapid clip, occasionally taking them two at a time in his haste.

When we reached the top of the stairs, he pushed his door open, and I got my first look at the duke's personal suite of rooms.

The room was furnished with lavish sage green rugs edged in a pink rose and gold pattern along the edges. Deeper green cushioned chairs clustered around a fireplace sporting a large, oak mantle that extended all the way to the ceiling in carved decorations, pillars, and a mirror. Wainscoting lined all the walls with pristine plaster above, painted in a soft green. A writing desk and a couch filled the wall across from the fireplace.

Across from us, a door had been set into the wall. Duke Guy strode toward it, not looking at me. "You may stay here if you wish."

In other words, he would be more uncomfortable if I followed him. So, of course, that was exactly what I would do.

As he stepped inside his bedchamber, I wandered inside after him.

This room too was carpeted with that soft green carpet. Keeping with the green theme, the bedspread was a deep, forest green while the four poster bed was a solid oak. Strangely, it was the most relaxing room I'd seen in this castle. Perhaps because all the green and oak reminded me of my beloved Greenwood.

The duke glanced over his shoulder at me before he

crossed the room and opened the door to a large, oak wardrobe. He reached inside, pulled out a long cloak nearly identical to the wet, dripping one he was wearing. He tossed it to me. "This should be warmer than what you are wearing."

I caught the cloak, my chilled fingers burying in the thick wool. This cloak was a rich blue, and I was thankful the color was so different from the drab brown-green cloak I wore as the Hood.

As I fumbled to remove my sodden cloak, Duke Guy rifled through his wardrobe again, pulling out and shutting a few drawers before he turned to me, holding one of his shirts and trousers. For the first time, his voice turned gruff, and his gaze looked at the floor rather than at me. "Here. Put these on with your dress. You'll stay warmer in the rain."

I gaped at him, finding myself truly befuddled and without a snappy comeback for once in my life.

He knelt before the trunk at the foot of his bed and lifted the lid, revealing a trunk full of swords, daggers, and other miscellaneous weapons.

At least I now knew the first place to raid when I ventured into his room.

He shuffled through the weapons before he pulled out a plain, but finely crafted knife in a sheath. After shutting the chest, he stood and faced me with the clothes in one hand, the knife in the other. "You'll need this too."

I raised my eyebrows at him. Little did he know how many weapons I had stashed in my room or how well I could use them. Not to mention the knife strapped to my leg under my dress. "What is this for?"

"I'm not well-liked in the village. I don't believe they will turn on you, but it would be best if you were armed." Still not looking at me, Duke Guy shoved the clothes and knife into my arms. "I'll see if the horses are ready."

With that, the duke hurried past me and disappeared out the door a second later, closing it firmly behind him.

I swung my gaze from the door to the knife and the bundle of clothes. That was beyond unexpected. What was his game in this? Surely he didn't actually have a care whether I caught a chill in this cold, autumn rain. Why would he care if I got sick if he was planning to kill me?

I shook myself, set the clothes on the trunk at the foot of his bed, and worked at the laces that held my other cloak in place. As tempting as it was to fully change into his clothes and leave my dress behind, that was a step too dangerous, even for a daredevil like me. Duke Guy had seen me dressed as the Hood. It might take him a while to put together the pieces of a niggling feeling, but he would get there eventually. I could not underestimate his intelligence.

Instead, I remained in my clammy, sticky dress and instead pulled the thick woolen trousers on underneath, the hem hanging only a little long. I tugged the shirt over my head and my dress. This garment sagged at the shoulders, and the sleeves drooped over my hands. It wasn't even tight in the chest since I was a flat stick—the only reason I could pull off my Hood disguise.

I attached the knife sheath to the sash of my dress. Not a great way to carry a knife, but it still felt right to be openly armed once again. With two knives on my person, I could take on just about anything.

When I threw on the cloak, I was enfolded in the warmth it provided. The smell of leather oil, beeswax, and spice clung to the clothing. It gave me a weak-kneed sensation, and I didn't like it.

I shook myself and strode toward the door. Whatever the smell of *him* in this clothing, it would quickly wash away in the rain.

After one last glance around his room to memorize its

layout, I left, hurrying down the staircase, through the trophy room at the tower's base, and once again stepped outside into the pouring rain.

Horses and wagons filled the castle courtyard, the clatter of many hooves on cobblestones echoed off the confining walls and towers of the castle.

In the center of the bustle, Duke Guy gripped the reins of his deep bay horse and gave additional orders, sending more servants and soldiers scrambling.

The soldiers and servants parted for me as I strode between them. When I reached the duke, I found a groom standing nearby, holding the reins of a gorgeous black horse. I found myself grinning despite the rain when the groom handed the reins over to me.

I ran my fingers over the black's nose, letting him get a good sniff of me. Even in the rain, he stood steady, and I liked that. I didn't need a fancy, high-stepper who would bolt at the wrong moment. A good, steady horse was much better for shooting from the saddle.

Not that I'd had a chance to practice that in the years since my parents had been killed. We were foresters, and our horses had been provided by the duke. Shortly after the duke inherited his title from his parents, he had reclaimed the horses when he dismissed us as foresters.

With an easy motion, I swung into the saddle, arranging my soggy skirts as best I could. At least the trousers I wore made it easier to sit astride. Odd that they hadn't saddled the horse with a sidesaddle. Still, I was grateful for that oversight, since I only knew how to ride astride and had never learned how to sit the ladylike sidesaddle.

Duke Guy also swung into the saddle. "I received word that the river is already rising."

"Then let's ride." I nudged the black with my heels.

En masse, we clattered out the castle's gate and cantered

down the cobbled road that led down the hill from the castle to the village below. Through the veil of rain, I squinted at the town ahead. Puddles already filled the road ahead of us while the river churned brown and frothy inside its banks. Not flooding. Yet.

As we reached the outskirts of town, Duke Guy gave orders to his men, making loading the wagons with the town's food stores the priority.

Townsfolk opened their doors and peered out. As soon as they caught sight of the duke and his soldiers swarming around the three large stone buildings that held the food stores, men from the village stepped from their homes, clenching their fingers as if they planned to take on the duke's soldiers with just their fists.

Bloodshed could break out, and I couldn't let the villagers do something foolish, as fear was often wont to do.

I rode my black horse over the bridge across the river into the town's main square, where I dismounted. More townsfolk were gathering, grumbling and muttering among themselves.

I straightened and faced them, putting the same command into my voice that I used when organizing my brothers. "I am Lady Robin, formerly of Loxsley and now lady of Gysborn." Funny how that was getting easier to say, as if somehow this new role was becoming just as much of my identity as the Hood was, even though neither of them were really who I was.

The townsfolk's muttering trailed off as they turned toward me, their hair flattening in the deluge.

I had to shout to be heard over the roaring river and pounding rain. "The river is already rising. The town is in danger of flooding, and you and your families must evacuate. The duke is also taking the precaution of moving the town's food supplies to the high ground of the castle."

"Where he can keep it for himself, most likely." The words were stated loudly enough that I could hear them, as if the townsfolk didn't care if their new lady overheard.

I understood their concerns, and I needed to reassure them. Not that they should trust the duke. Never that. But they had nothing to worry about because I, as the Hood, would not allow the duke to keep the food stores.

In my guise as Lady of Gysborn, I couldn't tell them that outright, nor would they believe me. Besides, there were too many soldiers nearby who could overhear.

As I swept my gaze around the town, blinking as rainwater ran into my eyes, I caught sight of both Will and John in the shadows of one of the houses. When I met Will's gaze, I gave him a slight nod. He would know what he would have to do.

He nudged John, then the two of them split up, murmuring to the townsfolk one-by-one. Those townsfolk leaned over to whisper to their neighbors, and as the word spread, the angry tension to the town disappeared. Some of the townsfolk even turned wide eyes on me, and it made me wonder what exactly my brothers had told them. Perhaps they had said something about Lady Robin of Loxsley working with the Hood. That was the logical thing, and what I would have told them, if I could speak freely.

With the townsfolk now in a more cooperative frame of mind, I set to work giving orders and organizing them. I sent each family off to their own homes to gather their things and ordered the soldiers to go from house to house to ask each family if they needed additional aid in packing. I caught glimpses of my brothers as they too helped the villagers in packing, but I didn't speak directly to them nor them with me.

Soon, a steady stream of people trudged up the hill through the downpour toward the castle, carrying their most prized possessions. Soldiers strode with them, carrying more of their belongings. Wagons rumbled, carrying the precious food stores that would see the village through the coming winter.

I strode through the village, checking each home and business and making sure everyone had evacuated successfully. The rain pounded so heavy and incessantly that it almost seemed unnatural. Perhaps that feeling was caused by such a rainstorm after going so long without rain.

The tunic and cloak the duke had given me were soaked through, sticking to my dress. My eyes burned as water flowed across my face, and I struggled to breathe through the sheer amount of rain gushing from the sky.

Even as we had been evacuating, the river had risen. It now lapped at the base of the bridge and spilled over the lower sections of the riverbanks, the water level roaring higher with each minute.

I urged the villagers to hurry. If that bridge washed out, then they would be trapped on that side of the river, cut off from the shelter of both the Greenwood and the castle.

As I hurried the last group of villagers across the bridge, an inch of water now covering the boards, Duke Guy halted next to me and gripped my arm. "We have to leave. That bridge is nearly underwater."

I took one last glance around, trying to peer through the thick veil of driving rain. I couldn't see any more villagers hurrying in our direction. Only the duke and his guards clustered around me.

With a nod, I let the duke lead the way toward the bridge. Even in the few seconds we had talked, the river had risen until a foot of water gushed over the bridge. As I stepped into the rush, one of my boots slipped, and I staggered. Duke Guy reached to steady me, then gripped the rail with his other hand as he slipped and went down to a knee.

BLUEBEARD AND THE OUTLAW

By instinct, I hauled him to his feet. Together, we slogged through the rushing water, even as the deluge continued from the dark clouds above. Everything was wet and cold and choked with rain.

At the far side of the bridge, hands reached to pull us the rest of the way to safety. When I glanced up, I found myself facing my brother John, his brown hair plastered to his head and rainwater running down his face.

Guards helped Duke Guy, and it tangled something inside me to see my brothers surrounded by guards, even if everyone was too focused on the flood to even think about capturing outlaws.

With a nod, John stepped back, fading into the rain to join the last few villagers who hadn't yet made their way to the castle.

Guards approached, leading the duke's bay horse and my black. As we reached for our horses' reins, a little girl raced out of the rain toward the river, shouting. It took me several minutes before I realized she was shouting a name. "Daisy! Daisy!"

I stepped away from my horse, hurrying toward the girl. If she got swept away by that roiling water, she would be long drowned by the time her body was found, if it ever was.

An answering bark came from the far side of the river, and a sodden, small dog raced out of the gloom, skidding to a halt inches from the water.

"Daisy!" The girl lunged, but I caught her before she could sprint onto the flooded bridge. She fought against me, and I had to haul her off her feet to keep her from wiggling free.

The dog's barking grew frantic as it raced back and forth at the edge of the churning river, its instincts knowing that stepping into that river would be a fatal mistake.

The girl was sobbing in my arms now. A man and a

woman sprinted toward me, and I guessed they had to be the girl's parents.

As I handed the girl to her mother, the duke's bay trotted past me, Duke Guy hunched on his horse's back. The horse snorted and pawed at the water, but it stepped onto the bridge at the duke's urging.

I held my breath, strangely worried for the duke's safety, as he coaxed his horse to trudge step by step across the bridge through the surging water. When he reached the far side, he dismounted, then crouched, trying to coax the panicked dog closer.

The dog raced back and forth for several more seconds, sniffing at the duke, then running away, getting a little closer each time. Finally, it came close enough that the duke snatched the dog by the ruff at the back of its neck.

The dog yipped and squirmed in the duke's grip. The duke tucked the wiggling dog under his arm, then remounted his horse, hugging the dog to him.

As he turned his horse back to the bridge, the wooden structure gave a deep groan.

Blast. The bridge wasn't going to hold. I would have to step in and try to save the duke. After all, I couldn't let the dog die. That was my only reason for risking my life.

I drew the knife he'd given me and hacked at the skirt of my dress. The wet fabric would only get in my way once I was in the water.

"My lady!" one of the nearby guards gasped, and another gaped. The rest were frozen, too busy staring at their lord as he started across the moaning bridge to pay any attention to me.

I dropped what was left of my skirt, standing there in the duke's trousers and his shirt clinging to me in the pouring rain. I took off the cloak as well. It wasn't doing anything to keep me dry, and the yards of wet wool would drag me down.

The bridge gave a shriek of twisting, cracking wood. The bay horse gave a high-pitched, horse scream of terror as it, Duke Guy, and the dog were plunged into the roiling water, surrounded by the jagged remains of the bridge. Logs battered the horse and the duke, who hunched over the dog to protect it.

Blast and bother. I snatched a length of rope from the saddle of one of the soldiers. I tied one end to the saddle of the black horse, then gestured from it to the soldiers. "Keep a hold of this."

The soldiers gaped at me before one of the soldiers grabbed the black's reins while others gripped the rope next to the horse.

In the river, the bay horse gamely swam across the rushing current. The duke had lost hold of the reins and gripped the dog with both arms, trying to keep the panicking creature still.

I tied the other end of the rope around my waist, then looped the rest of it over my shoulder. With a bracing breath, I plunged into the river. The current caught me, dragging me downstream.

I struggled to angle myself toward the duke and his horse, fighting the roiling water. I had strong arms from many years of archery, yet those muscles strained as I worked to pull myself through the flood.

Finally, my grasping hand touched the bay's warm, water-slicked coat. Scrabbling, I grabbed its reins, then angled myself alongside the horse to avoid getting in the way of its flailing legs.

I tugged a loop of the rope out of the water and held it out to the duke. He didn't try to talk but took the rope and wrapped it tightly around the saddle's horn.

As the rope tightened, he kept a grip on the rope, holding it in place as it tugged at the horse. I swam alongside, gripping the reins and urging the exhausted horse onward.

The horse staggered, then lunged as its hooves found the bottom. I clung to it, letting the horse pull me free of the water. When the horse was all the way on the bank, it halted, head hanging as it heaved panting breaths.

I sagged against it, also gasping for breath. We'd survived.

The duke swung down from the horse, landing on the ground beside me with the squirming dog still gripped in his arms. His dark gaze focused on me. "Are you crazy?"

"Are you?" I shot back, starting to shake from cold and exhaustion.

He glanced down to the dog in his arms, then shrugged. "I suppose I must be."

"Daisy!" The girl's cry of joy set the dog to wiggling again a moment before three figures appeared out of the veil of rain, the little girl in the lead.

The duke set down the dog, and it raced to the girl, its tail wagging so hard that its whole body wriggled with the movement. It flung itself into the girl's arms, licking her face and her hands and any part of exposed skin.

"Please come, my lord, my lady." One of the soldiers approached us, his gaze focused on Duke Guy. "You need to get dry and warm."

With a nod, the duke gripped his horse's reins and strode in the direction of the castle. He was limping, and I could see small gashes on the horse's flank. Both of them would need medical attention.

But, for a moment, I could only stare after them. I had married the duke intending to kill him. I had shot several arrows in his direction. Perhaps it would have solved all my problems if I had simply stood by and let him drown.

Yet, when the time had come, I had thrown myself into

the river without thinking about it. Sure, I could tell myself that I had done it to save the dog and the horse. But I wasn't the type to do nothing while someone drowned, even if that person was the duke. If he was killed, it would be because he was actively trying to kill me.

Even that grated inside me, as if the pieces of what I'd always believed about the duke no longer fit together.

He had risked his life to save a little girl's dog. Was that the action of a cruel man? A man who would murder his wives?

Maybe so.

Even a murderer could be kind to a dog.

Chapter Six

I was torn. I had saved the duke's life, yet I still planned to kill him. That wasn't a comfortable place to be in, especially as I played the lady of the castle and saw to the care of the villagers while they waited for the rain to stop and the flood to recede.

No matter his actions in saving the dog, I had to stay focused. One day, he was going to try to kill me, and I couldn't afford to hesitate when the time came to kill him first. I might be a woman drawn to danger, but risking my heart was one danger from which even I fled.

As the early dawn sunlight filtered through the windows behind me, I shuffled through the papers on the duke's desk. There were calculations on how bad the harvest would be due to both the drought and the past week of flooding, estimations of how much food would have to be imported to feed the village and castle folk, how much importing that food would cost, and how much the king intended to tax the people to cover this.

All very interesting, but not what I was looking for. After extensive exploration of the castle, I had finally found a hallway of what appeared to be vaults in the lower levels of the castle under the tower with the magical creature mounts and the secretive door. The vaults too had the lingering sense of fae magic, just like the small door.

But the area was so well guarded and patrolled that I hadn't had a chance to pick the locks and sneak into the rooms. Unless I had a distraction to draw away the guards, I wasn't getting into those vaults.

The duke's desk sat with its back to a bank of four windows, shining plenty of early morning light onto the papers before me now that the rain had finally stopped. Bookshelves covered the wall to my left from floor to ceiling while the door to the room was set across from the desk.

To my right, the second half of the room was more casual with a large fireplace, several cushioned chairs, and a sideboard that held brandy and glasses.

I growled and tapped the papers into the neat stacks they had been in originally. Nothing to tell me how much wealth was hidden in those vaults. Nor any information on what kind of magical fae booby-traps the duke might have laid for anyone trying to steal his riches. I had been married to him for a week, and I had little to show for it.

Footsteps and voices came from the hall outside the study. I froze, my breath catching as the duke's deep tones rumbled through the closed door.

Blast. He normally spent the mornings drilling with his guards and patrolling the forest. He shouldn't be here.

I didn't have time to waste wondering *why* he was there. The important thing was that he was headed for his study, and I needed to hide.

I glanced under the desk, then quickly dismissed it. If the

duke came around this side of the desk, he would see me in a heartbeat.

The bookshelves provided no shelter. I didn't have time to climb out the window.

The sideboard crouched along the center of the wall to my right, leaving a shadowed corner between it and the wall. One of the cushioned chairs from the fireplace was set only a foot in front of that corner, leaving a space where I could crouch. I had chosen a deep gray dress since I had been planning to snoop, and it would thankfully blend into the stones of the wall.

It wasn't the best hiding place. If the duke walked over to that sideboard for a glass of brandy, then I would be spotted.

I had no other choice.

As the doorknob rattled, I raced across the room, the wool carpet muffling the boots I was wearing beneath my dress, and I flung myself over the chair arm and dropped into the corner. I curled into the corner as the door swung open.

I pressed my face against the back of the chair where my pale face and hair would be hidden. While it was tempting to peek out, I resisted the urge. If I could see them, then they could see me if they looked in my direction. At this point, movement on my part would draw their notice.

The door clicked shut, then muffled sounds of boots on the carpet stalked across the room. The chair I had vacated creaked, and I hoped the leather had cooled to the point that the new occupant couldn't tell someone else had recently been there.

Another chair gave the groan of shifting wood and leather as another person sat across from the desk. Then, Sheriff Reinhault's tenor pierced the tense silence. "You should give me free rein. Your king is not pleased at your recent failure to protect the tax shipment. This summons to

BLUEBEARD AND THE OUTLAW

his court might be the king's attempt to find a way to remove you as duke."

They were talking about that last heist I had pulled off before marrying the duke. In the week and a half since then, word of that theft must have reached the king and now his answering summons had been sent back to the duke to take him to task in person for his failures.

I probably shouldn't feel so gleeful at the thought of the duke squirming before the king.

"He won't. He can't." Duke Guy's deep voice had a firmness to it. Almost a warning. Why? Did he think he could threaten the king to prevent his removal?

He did have a point. The king might want to replace the duke, but even he might not have that power. No matter how much Duke Guy might be reviled by his fellow dukes, barons, and lords throughout the kingdom, they would band together to protect him and his position if the king tried to remove him. The other lords wouldn't want to give the king the power to remove any of them at will.

"Perhaps he can't. But he can send his soldiers to occupy your castle while leaving you as a powerless figurehead." Sheriff Reinhault's voice lowered, though it was still audible from my crouched position behind the chair. "That is something I can't allow."

"No, I suppose you can't." Duke Guy heaved a weary sigh, and I could almost see him rubbing his temples as he seemed wont to do. "Then what do you suggest I do? This outlaw has been a thorn in my side for years. That isn't going to change by the time I face the king. Are you sure he isn't a fae? He seems to make use of the faerie circles with impunity."

I let myself smirk, since I was fully hidden behind the chair. No, not a fae. Just a woman well-trained in the faerie paths by her forester parents.

"I do not believe he is fae. But his use of the circles is curious." Sheriff Reinhault trailed off, as if thinking. "Perhaps you need a success to present to the king. If you delay your departure by a few days, you can take the time to trap the Hood."

"The king will not be pleased if I delay in answering his summons." The duke's deepening tone revealed that even someone infamous still feared the king.

"If you fail, then, yes, the king will have yet one more thing for which to call you to account." Sheriff Reinhault's voice smoothed into an even richer tenor. "But if you can succeed in capturing the Hood, then you will arrive at the king's castle in triumph instead of disgrace."

Duke Guy gave a long sigh, as if giving in beneath the sheriff's pressure. "It would not be too unusual, given the coming harvest, that I would delay a few days to make sure all was progressing well before I reported to the king. But our plan to capture the Hood must succeed, otherwise my situation with the king will be dire."

"Of course." Sheriff Reinhault's chair squeaked, as if he was leaning forward. "Then we will have to set a trap from which this outlaw can't escape. We must lure him out of his forest and his faerie circles."

"Get him out of his home territory into ours." Duke Guy's tone turned thoughtful. "Perhaps an archery tournament, held here in the castle courtyard."

"Do you think the outlaw would dare step foot in the castle, no matter the prize we offer?" I could almost picture Sheriff Reinhault shaking his head, his long blond queue brushing across his shoulders. "Perhaps the village would be better? It is more neutral."

"Oh, he would dare. The Hood loves a good challenge too much to resist." Duke Guy's voice held a trace of a growl. "Besides, the villagers love the outlaw far too well. They would readily hide him from our men, should we try to apprehend him there. The love of the people is one of the weapons he uses so easily against us."

I resisted the urge to shift. It was uncomfortable, hearing the duke read me so well.

No, not me. My persona as the Hood. It was part of the disguise I had built over the years, using parts of my personality to build a legend rather than a real person.

Still, the duke was right. This was a challenge the Hood wouldn't turn down. As the duke and the sheriff discussed the details of their trap, my heart beat harder with the anticipation of the thrill. What an adventure it would be, winning the contest right under the nose of the duke!

Surely I could pull it off. After all, he thought he was taking the Hood out of his home in the forest onto the foreign territory of the castle.

But since my marriage to the duke, this castle was my home territory as much as the forest. I had more weapons and advantages than the duke realized.

AT SUPPER, I struggled to pretend to be surprised as the duke described the upcoming archery contest while we were slurping our soup course. Sheriff Reinhault wasn't there, leaving just the two of us at the head of the long table. My plate had been set to the duke's left, as was usual after my stunt on my first day here.

"It sounds like it will be a fun reprieve for the village after the flooding." I kept my tone neutral as I stirred what remained of my soup. The villagers had just returned to the town, and they were in the process of rebuilding the bridge.

If I hadn't known that the archery contest was a trap for the Hood, I would question why the duke was using his resources on an archery contest rather than on rebuilding efforts.

"Yes." The duke's flat tone didn't seem to agree with me, exactly. It was almost like he didn't approve of wasting time and energy on his own archery contest. "That is why I would like you to help organize it."

I struggled to hold back my grin. He was making it just too easy, asking for my help to plan the trap for myself. I should have realized that he might ask, given that I was now the lady of Gysborn. In the past week, I had stepped into that role as we cared for the villagers taking shelter here at the castle while we all waited for the rain to cease and the flooding to dissipate.

I forced my tone and posture to remain casual. "I will do my best. A contest sounds like a lovely day. Perhaps we will invite traveling entertainers and put a wide call for archers. We might as well make a festival of it."

"Whatever you wish." Duke Guy dipped his spoon into his vegetable soup. "I should tell you, this contest is a trap for the outlaw the Hood."

I choked on my swallow of soup and coughed. I hadn't expected the duke to actually confide in me.

His heavy gaze rested on me. "I didn't mean to distress you. His attack on your traveling party was a traumatic experience for you."

Oh, right. He assumed I was coughing because I had been traumatized by the Hood's supposed attack on my way here. I feigned a weak nod as I kept coughing to clear my lungs.

"During the archery contest, if you see the Hood, please point him out to Sheriff Reinhault, one of the guards, or me. We will make sure he never hurts you again." Duke Guy's expression turned soft, almost gentle.

I hated it when he turned all caring and compassionate. It

made it so much harder to stay focused on killing him when he eventually tried to kill me.

"I'm sure you'll keep me safe." I tried to say that with a straight face. Even if I hadn't been the Hood, the famed outlaw would only rob me. The duke would kill me. Of the two, the duke clearly posed the greater threat. I met the duke's gaze and tried to appear innocent. "Are you sure the Hood is that much of a threat? Yes, he robbed me. But he claims to be an honorable man who is fighting for the villagers."

The duke snorted and lounged against the back of his chair. "Don't tell me that you have bought into that outlaw's propaganda?"

"Propaganda? Is that what you think it is?" I pushed my soup bowl away and leaned my elbows on the table. I was genuinely curious. I had fought the duke as the Hood for years, yet this was the first time I could sit down and hear his side of that battle.

"Yes, propaganda. That outlaw claims to be honorable, but an honorable man doesn't skulk in the shadows robbing tax collections and innocent travelers. An honorable man works hard, providing for his family and for others by the work of his hands. He doesn't steal from the hard work of others." Duke Guy's face hardened, his dark eyes turning as flinty as his voice. "He claims to fight for the people, but with every robbery, he makes life worse for them."

That stabbed me through my core. Surely not. Duke Guy was simply blinded by his own greed and hatred of everything that the Hood fought for. He claimed to respect the hard work of others, but he was the one getting rich by taxing them more than they could pay. He was the one who forced me into this.

I swallowed, but my voice still came out slightly rough. "How so?"

"With every tax shipment that the outlaw takes, the more soldiers the king sends to guard the next one." Duke Guy's jaw flexed beneath his thick beard. "And the king won't provide those soldiers for free. Instead, he raises the taxes on Gysborn to pay for the men he is forced to send."

No. No, that couldn't be it at all. Surely I wasn't making things worse. The villagers loved the Hood too much for me to be making things worse for them.

Besides, I had become the Hood back before the king had started sending soldiers. Duke Guy had already been raising taxes long before the king started doing so.

"And you place that extra tax burden on the poor villagers rather than taking it on yourself?" I couldn't help the heat in my voice. Perhaps it was dangerous, giving away so much of my passion for this topic. But if I was lucky, the duke would chalk it up to the bonding I had done with the villagers in this past week while they sheltered at the castle.

For the first time since we started this conversation, the duke looked away. "It is not that simple. There is a right and a wrong way to do things, and this outlaw's way is wrong."

I resisted the urge to roll my eyes. Of course it wouldn't seem that simple to him. Yet, the simple truth was that he was too greedy to use any of his own wealth to pay the taxes. He could condemn me for helping the villagers in the wrong way, but he was certainly not a better man than the Hood.

Didn't the king realize what he was doing by continually raising the taxes? It was human nature to hold on to wealth. The greedy wouldn't take those taxes onto themselves but would pass the real cost of the taxes to those below them.

I hardened my resolve. Perhaps he was partially right, and my continued raids were contributing to the problem. A good reason why this needed to be my final heist.

But I wasn't the source of the problem. Duke Guy was. I had to bring him down once and for all. It didn't matter if I

BLUEBEARD AND THE OUTLAW

had seen glimmers of honor such as the way he had sheltered the villagers and his heroics in saving the dog Daisy.

In his heart, he must be cruel. There was no other explanation for the way he had been taxing the villagers so harshly for so long.

THAT EVENING, I dressed in my Hood disguise, including leather gloves, tied the rope to a bedpost, then dropped the end out the window. I walked down the tower wall using the rope, and I reached the ground in less than a minute. After tucking the end of the rope into a shrub growing at the base of the wall where it would be less noticeable should a guard walk by, I set out into the darkness toward the forest.

Once the cool darkness of the Greenwood closed around me, I started whistling as I sauntered between the trees. After days of being locked inside stone walls, always on guard surrounded by my enemies, my muscles relaxed as I strolled through the forest. This was home.

As I neared the hideout spot that was closest to the duke's castle, an answering whistle came from the darkness ahead a moment before a figure dropped from a tree.

Munch's voice came from the blackness. "Robin? What are you doing here?"

"I have news to report, so I sneaked out of the castle." I reached his side, so thankful to see one of my brothers safe and sound that I bumped my shoulder into his hard enough to send him staggering a step. "Are the others all here?"

Munch nodded, his head just a black silhouette against the dark forest. "We've been waiting for you to give the signal."

As hard as it was, spending time in the castle surrounded by the duke, the sheriff, and guards who would gladly arrest me if they knew who I was, it must be worse for my brothers, waiting here in the Greenwood with nothing to do and no way of knowing what was happening.

As I pushed through the dense screen of underbrush, a faint glow filled the forest before I stepped into the orange light of the low-burning fire. My brothers sat on logs around the fire, though they jumped to their feet as I threw back my hood.

"Robin!" Will rushed to me, but it was John who got to me first. He wrapped me in a hug, lifting me off my feet.

I chuckled my loud, booming laugh that I didn't dare let loose while pretending to be a lady back there at the castle. "Set me down!"

As soon as John placed me back on my feet, Will gripped my shoulders, sweeping his gaze up and down as if searching for injuries. "Are you truly all right? Has he tried to kill you?"

Munch, Marion, Tuck, and Alan all crowded in behind him and John.

"No, not yet. Which has been rather disappointing." I grimaced and patted the knife at my side. "He mostly avoids me."

"That's a good thing." Will's grip tightened on my shoulders. "You shouldn't sound so annoyed by that."

"Of course, I'm annoyed! It's making it terribly tricky to wheedle information out of him." I extracted myself out of Will's grip, only to be swept up in Alan's hug instead.

After being passed from Alan to Tuck's back-pounding and Marion's awkward I'm-glad-you're-not-dead half-hug, I finally pulled free. I gestured to the logs around the fire. "But I managed to find out something useful this morning while I was snooping through the duke's study."

Munch and Marion sat promptly, and Tuck, Alan, and John started in that direction. But Will lingered, still studying me. "Did you find something in his paperwork?"

"No, his papers were basically useless." I pushed past Will and swept my cloak out of the way before I lounged on the nearest log. "It was what I overheard when the duke and the sheriff came into the room while I was still in there."

"What?" Will's voice rose an octave from behind me. "Did they catch you?"

"Obviously not." I gestured to the last remaining log. "Come on, Will, sit down and let me talk."

"Look at her. She's fine. And she's got that smirk of hers that says this plan is going to be good." Alan rolled his eyes. "Now stop dallying so the rest of us can hear it."

"*Good* isn't what I'd call most of her plans." Will grumbled, but he plopped onto the log, leaned his elbows on his knees, and went silent.

Quickly, I summarized the location of the treasure vaults below the tower and what I had overheard.

Will dropped his head into his hands. "You want to enter, don't you?"

"Of course." I pressed a hand over my heart. "Faint hearts never robbed a duke of all his treasure."

Will just groaned. "Fine, fine. Just please tell me you don't intend to do this all by yourself."

"No, this is an adventure for all of my merry men." I propped a boot on one of the outer stones around the fire, warming my toes as the autumn night turned crisp and cold around us.

Grinning, John gripped his quarterstaff with both hands. "How do we pull this off?"

"Oh, that part is going to be easy." I leaned my elbows on my knees. "The duke put me in charge of planning it. At least, the archery contest part. He is planning the trap part."

Will just sighed and shook his head. John slapped his knee, grinning. Munch and Marion both shook with their chuckles while Tuck waggled his ladle at me.

Alan threw back his head and laughed so hard he nearly fell off his log. "Only you, Robin, would be put in charge of planning a trap for yourself."

I smirked back at all of them. "It's going to be my greatest performance yet."

Chapter Seven

Yes, we come to it at last. The famous archery contest, and its prize of a golden arrow. And a kiss, if you believe some of the stories.

You might be wondering how I managed to pull off being both Lady Robin and the Hood during the contest without Duke Guy starting to wonder why his wife kept disappearing any time the Hood was around.

That part was almost too easy. All I had to do was play up a bit of internal discomfort, mumble something about returning to my room for the rest of the day because it was (embarrassed cough) that time, and presto, I had an alibi no man would question. Ever. Besides, the duke had been married three times. He wasn't some innocent youth blithely ignorant of the way the world worked.

What? Did you really think I would duck back and forth, frantically changing my clothes every couple of minutes?

Pfft. Amateurs.

I strolled into the Greenwood, dressed in ratty black trousers and a ragged red shirt with my quiver at my hip and unstrung bow across my back. The garb was different enough from the brown-and-green I wore as the Hood that hopefully it would take the duke and the sheriff a little longer to spot me.

Only a few yards into the forest, Will and Tuck stepped out from behind trees. They were also wearing ragged peasants' garb, complete with floppy hats that obscured their faces.

Will held out a black hat with a floppy brim to me. "Are you sure about this, Rob?"

"Definitely." I pulled the hat over my hair, making sure my braid was fully covered. I probably should have cut my hair long ago, but I was allowed one feminine vanity. Besides, I never wouldn't have gained the advantage of marrying the duke if I had chopped my hair.

My heart was beating, my chest twisting. This was going to be such an audacious adventure. A thrill the likes of which I had not had the opportunity to experience. Winning an archery contest right under the nose of the duke—my husband. Evading his trap.

Today was going to be *fun*.

I held out my hand to Tuck. "Did you bring it?"

Tuck held out a black eyepatch. "Wearing this is going to make winning more difficult."

As an archer, I shot with both eyes open and focused on the target, calculating trajectory through years of practice. The eyepatch would throw off my depth perception and make it that much harder to shoot accurately.

I secured the eyepatch over my left eye, blinking several times as I adjusted to the change in my vision. "I don't have to win. I just have to draw out the contest long enough for the rest of you to raid the treasure vaults."

Will huffed a sigh. "I know you, Robin. You're here to win, even if it doesn't matter in the grand scheme of things."

He had me there. Sure, I was looking forward to my brothers pulling off this heist and stealing the duke's gold. And, yes, the contest itself would be quite the lark.

But it wouldn't be a true challenge if I didn't make it a little harder on myself. My brothers and I had practiced over the years shooting with one eye closed. It had been a while since I'd done it, but I would remember that old skill soon enough.

Besides, I had to do something to alter my face since I couldn't wear my hood. I had spent far too much time in the duke's presence over the past two weeks. He could recognize me much easier now than he could before.

Since the thing I was looking forward to the most was bantering with the duke while I out-shot him, I needed a disguise that would let me get close enough for talking.

Finally, I glued on the fake mustache, completing my transformation to the Hood. I grinned at my two brothers. "Time to lead the duke on a merry chase."

Will rolled his eyes, but both he and Tuck fell into step behind me as I sauntered through the edge of the forest toward the open castle gates.

At the gates, we joined the crowd of people entering the castle. The guards' gaze swept over us, probably noting our bows and quivers, but they didn't hassle us. That was part of both my plan and the duke's plot. He wanted to lure the Hood and his men into the castle. I wanted to smuggle my brothers inside so that they could rob the castle.

The courtyard bustled with people. A large roped-off area surrounded by guards marked the archery range with the targets set on one end and a wooden pavilion built at the other end, complete with a canopy and chairs where the sheriff and the duke would sit. There was an empty chair for me that must have been put there before they learned Lady Robin wouldn't be making an appearance. Everyone else would watch standing in a packed crowd along the ropes on either side.

For now, the crowd milled about, enjoying the treats the castle kitchen had managed to scrape together from our supplies without risking starvation through this coming winter. The pleasant sound of music came from a cluster of people. As they shifted, I caught a glimpse of Alan, dressed in a flamboyant costume, as he strummed a lute and sang a popular folk tune about a tragic romance.

At the center of another cluster of people near the castle's stables, John, Munch, and Marion were also dressed in flamboyant costumes as they tumbled and flipped and performed as a traveling tumbling troupe. Based on the clapping of the crowd, they were doing a good job for a group of unprofessionals.

With Will and Tuck trailing me, I pushed through the crowd and joined the end of the line to sign up for the archery contest. Thankfully, the line moved quickly, and soon I stood before a table. A guard sat behind it, a pen and piece of paper in front of him. No flicker of recognition crossed his face as he stared up at me. "Name?"

"Nat the Blinker." I drawled the name in my deeper voice. "'Cause of the eyepatch."

The guard gave a grunt and wrote down the moniker. "Next."

Well, he had no sense of humor. What was this place coming to if people didn't laugh when I made a joke about my own appearance?

I stepped aside, waiting while both Will and Tuck added fake names to the list. Once we had all signed up, we faded into the crowd, working our way to a quiet corner near the stables.

Soon, Marion, Munch, and John joined us, still dressed in their vibrant clothing. After only a few more minutes, Alan strolled into our corner, his lute now tucked into a case on his back.

"All right, everyone, here's the plan." I handed them each a map of the castle that I'd drawn. "John, Marion, Munch, I stashed servants' clothing for each of you in the stables. Head for the lower floors of the castle. Alan, you'll stand watch for them. Tuck and Will, you'll stick with me until you're eliminated from the contest, then you'll help the others. When you're done, hide out in my room. I'll meet you there."

With all the servants and guards emptied into the courtyard for the day, it was the perfect opportunity for my brothers to finally rob the duke's treasure vault.

A trumpet sounded, signaling the end of the entertainment and the beginning of the archery contest.

While Alan, Munch, Marion, and John slipped inside the stables, Will, Tuck, and I worked our way into the crowd of other archers waiting for our name to be called for our turn to shoot.

Duke Guy and Sheriff Reinhault sat in their seats on the pavilion, my chair conspicuously empty. Duke Guy's hard, dark gaze studied the pack of archers, skipping from man to man as if noting them for the future.

The duke's black hair and beard were meticulously in place, glinting with a deep blue-black sheen. He wore a blue shirt and black trousers with quality leather braces, leather tunic, and matching knee-high boots. The quiver and unstrung bow showed that he intended to compete in his own tournament, something he'd noised about as an enticement to the Hood.

Not that he'd needed that extra incentive, but he didn't

know that.

With all the leather and his bow, he cut a strong, tall figure, complete with dark brooding eyes deep set above prominent cheekbones and a jaw that I could only guess was as strong as the rest of his facial features, though his beard obscured the shape.

My heart lurched in a way I'd never felt before. It was kind of like the thrill of an arrow passing close to my head, almost-death and precious-life all at once. My instincts screamed danger, yet that same danger lured me toward it anyway.

I had never thought I would be drawn to any man. I was too independent. Too much my own person. Too unwilling to make the sacrifices necessary to stand at the side of anyone else.

Perhaps we could have become something. If I had been someone other than myself—an outlaw, a leader, a woman drawn to danger. And if he had been someone other than himself—a murderer, a duke, a man given to cruelty.

But, we weren't, and thus we never could be.

As his gaze swung toward me, I lazily tipped my head, placing the floppy edge of my hat between him and me. I could feel the intensity of his gaze lingering on me. My heart pounded harder, and it took all my discipline to stop myself from giving the duke a salute.

The weight of his gaze moved beyond me as the herald called out the first set of names.

I tried not to pace as each set of archers strode to the line and took their turns shooting. While I knew my brothers needed all the time this contest could give them, I wanted the reckless thrills to begin. Waiting was dead boring.

The herald called the duke's name, and Duke Guy strode confidently down the stairs of the pavilion to take his place in the line of archers.

I leaned forward onto my toes. Now this was something I wanted to see. Duke Guy had shot at me numerous times, coming close enough to hitting his target to tell me he was good with that bow.

For the sake of my disguise, I should be hoping that he would get eliminated.

But I wasn't. That reckless streak of mine had me all tied up in knots hoping this contest would come down to me and Duke Guy. It wouldn't be as much fun if I faced down some innocent archer who had just come for a bit of prize money.

When it was his turn, Duke Guy raised his bow and drew back the nocked arrow with a perfect, fluid motion. The strength of his muscles was apparent as his shirt and leather vest pulled taut around his shoulders.

My mouth went strangely dry, my head a touch light. A monster like him had no right to look that good while handling a bow and arrow.

When the duke released, the arrow flew true, striking just inside the line marking the center circle.

"Robin." Will gave me a sharp nudge with his elbow, his whisper harsh. "Don't look at him like that."

I blinked, my vision going blurry as I adjusted to seeing through only one eye. I had to fully turn to look at Will. "Like what?"

Will's jaw flexed. "Like you find him attractive."

As I couldn't hide the fact that I had been staring, I gave a nonchalant shrug, keeping my voice lowered so that those around us wouldn't hear. "What can I say? I'm attracted to dangerous things. But don't worry. I'm very good at putting arrows in monsters when the time comes."

Though, it would be a pity when it happened. Duke Guy was deadly. He taxed the villagers harshly and killed his wives. But a part of me would mourn when our game was over. After all, a hero was only as good as her nemesis.

"You'd better be." Will's grip tightened on his bow as he stared me down.

Tuck shifted, his fingers flexing as if he was wishing he held his ladle instead of a bow.

Finally, my fake name was called, and I sauntered to my place in line. As the others shot one-by-one, I took a moment to study the target affixed to the front of a stack of hay bales two-thirds of the way across the courtyard, trying to judge the distance as best as I could with my left eye covered by the eyepatch.

Almost lazily, I opened the cover to my quiver just enough to withdraw one of the white-fletched practice arrows. Instead of the large, barbed broadhead that I would use on a deer or a man, the practice arrow had a small iron tip that would be easy to remove from the hay bale for reuse. I let the cover of my quiver fall back in place to keep my black-fletched, deadlier arrows hidden from sight.

Nocking the arrow, I drew it back as I raised the bow, my back and shoulders working together. I focused on the target, letting out my breath before holding it for just a single, steadying instant as I released.

The arrow hissed through the air, slicing into the target on the line that marked the center circle and disappearing into the hay bale up to the fletching.

I scowled at the arrow. It had been a decent shot. Good enough to ensure that I advanced to the next round. But it had not been my best, and I would need to improve my accuracy shooting with this eyepatch if I hoped to defeat the duke in the final round.

Will and Tuck each took their own turns at shooting. Will buried his arrow only a hair short of the center, and when I turned, I could see the way both the duke and the sheriff straightened and started watching him more closely.

I knew Will had done that on purpose, drawing their

attention away from me. And I really shouldn't have been miffed that he'd managed a better first shot than I had.

Tuck, however, ended up in a group of skilled archers from several villagers over, and he was eliminated. They would be a group to watch, as they had the potential to knock the duke or me out of the contest if either of us slipped up.

By the second round, I had adjusted to the eyepatch enough that I put my arrow well inside the center circle. In both the third and fourth rounds, I had found my stride, putting my arrows through the center dot both times. That made me the focus of the duke, the sheriff, and the spectators.

The duke had also survived his rounds, placing his arrows near the center dot, and once through it. With each shot, he kept glancing between me and Will more often, as if trying to decide which of the two of us was the Hood. I had to keep my floppy hat pulled low and my left side toward him.

By the time we reached the sixth, semi-final round, it was down to me, the duke, Will, and one of the skilled archers from the town down the river. The crowd around us cheered and kept up a steady roar of discussion, and they had to have figured out by now that one of the three archers who found themselves facing the duke in this round had to be their hero, the Hood.

As the target was moved back another few paces, the four of us lined up with the duke on the far end. We were down to a single target set on hay bales ahead of us.

Will selected his arrow, not looking at me. "I'm not going to throw this round, you know."

"I don't expect you to." I also picked through my practice arrows until I found one that felt especially right in my hand. Regardless of my role as the Hood, Will was first and foremost my brother. And brothers didn't just let their sister win without making her work awfully hard for it. Nor would I want him to do anything less.

The duke raised his bow first, pausing a moment before he let his arrow fly. It slammed into the target just a hair to the side of the center dot. A very good shot, but beatable.

The skilled archer from a few villagers over lifted his bow, took a moment, and released. Perhaps it was nerves. Maybe he paused too long. Or it was just the lot of any archer that a shot is bound to go astray every once and while. But this time, the stranger's arrow thunked into the line around the center circle. By the way the man's shoulders slumped, he knew that it was unlikely he'd progress to the final round.

Now it was my turn. I nocked the arrow and drew, my muscles steadying with the familiar feel of my bow flexing, the string taut against the leather guard on the fingers of my right hand. A whiff of a breeze brushed my cheek, and I added that to my swift, mental instincts.

I released. My arrow hissed, then slammed into the target in the center dot, so close to the duke's arrow that our two shafts scraped against each other.

The archer from out of town bowed and strode out of line, acknowledging that he was out of the contest.

Next to me, Will's mouth pressed into a tight line. The best he could do now was put his arrow as close to mine as the duke's was and force a re-shoot to determine which of them would move to the final round.

With a deep breath, Will drew back his arrow, then released. His arrow flew through the air and pierced the target a mere half an inch below my arrow. Another great shot, but not close enough to beat the duke.

Will shook his head, flicking his glance toward me and muttering below his breath. "Looks like you got your way. As usual. Don't do anything too reckless."

With that, Will faded into the crowd. A few of the soldiers moved, as if they planned to stop him, but the duke gave a small shake of his head.

Good. He was waiting to close in on me, leaving Will free to move about for now. Will would most likely be watched, but he would know to handle that little inconvenience.

I struggled to suppress my grin, a surging laugh building inside my chest until it was almost painful. It was down to me and Duke Guy, just as it was always meant to be.

Four soldiers hurried onto the range to move the hay bales back by a few more feet until they were set all the way up against the far castle wall. Another soldier replaced the shot-up target with a freshly painted target cloth, affixing it to the hay bales with a great deal of care so that it lay flat and taut. There could be no mistakes, no detail left overlooked, for this final round.

I heard the duke's bootsteps crunch on the cobblestones as he stepped closer to me until we stood only a few feet apart at the line. But I didn't turn my head to look at him, keeping the side with the eyepatch facing him.

"Hood." He ground the word between his teeth as if it was a curse.

"We meet again, Duke Bluebeard." I used the village's derogatory name on purpose, knowing it would rile him.

"You're surrounded. You won't get away this time. Save us the trouble and surrender." Duke Guy's tone was flint.

"And let you hang me without so much as a fight? I think not." I laughed and gestured toward the target, sitting alone at the far end now that the soldiers had hurried out of the way. "The people came for a show. Let's give it to them, shall we?"

"Fine." The timbre of the duke's snarl changed as he turned to face the target instead of me. "Enjoy your last free moments, Hood. You will not leave this castle."

I gave another laugh as I selected my arrow. I had no intention of leaving. This was my castle, even if he didn't know it. "I wish you luck. Bad luck."

"By all means, Hood. I wish you the same." Out of the corner of my uncovered right eye, I could see the tip of his arrow as he raised his bow.

I smirked. How I would miss this banter with him when I was forced to kill him. The dukedom would be a much more boring place without him in it.

With that same, fluid motion, the duke drew his arrow back, his bow bending in a swelling curve in his strong hands. He released after only a heartbeat with the confidence of a skilled archer.

The arrow sailed through the air, straight and true, taking the target in the dead center.

I caught my breath, a momentary weight settling into my chest. His had been a great shot. An unbeatable shot.

The duke's voice held a smirk, even if I didn't turn to see it. "I hope you aren't too disappointed. It seems you won't have the pleasure of holding the golden arrow before I hang you."

That golden arrow was *mine*. I had picked it out specifically for *me*. There was no way I was letting the duke claim it.

Out of the corner of my uncovered eye, I could just see the duke's hand as he gestured from me to the target. "Perhaps you wish to surrender now, Hood, before you have to endure the humiliation of losing an archery contest to me."

Fat chance of that. I was going to win this thing yet, see if I didn't.

Around us, the crowd had gone deathly silent. They, too, realized that their hero was on the verge of defeat. An edge of despair curled around them as the grandiose legend I'd built around the Hood crumbled when faced with reality.

They expected the impossible out of me. Then *impossible* was exactly what I was going to give them.

This time, I tossed back the covering of my quiver, revealing the fletching of my arrows for all to see. It didn't matter at this point. The duke knew I was the Hood. His guards were poised to snatch me as soon as I completed this shot.

Sweet, sweet danger. It rushed through my chest, my veins, so heady I was nearly dizzy with it.

I slid the practice arrow I had selected back into my quiver, and instead trailed my fingers over the black-fletching until my fingers brushed one that resonated with me. I drew the arrow from the quiver, its large iron broadhead winking in the early afternoon sunlight.

A collective gasp came from the crowd, the silence stretching into one of anticipation instead of the despair of a moment earlier. The duke muttered something under his breath. Perhaps cursing my audacity.

Then, the world narrowed to me, my bow, my arrow, and the far-off target. The bow bent to my will, the arrow lifting. I sank into my instincts, lifting the tip of the arrow as demanded by my years of practice and those honed, uncanny senses gifted to me by the hint of fae blood that ran through my veins.

I breathed in, my hands steady, my muscles strong. I slowly exhaled part of the breath out, then I uncurled my fingers, releasing the arrow.

It whistled through the air before it struck with a splintering crack.

For a heartbeat, no one moved. It was almost as if no one even dared breathe as we stared at my black-fletched arrow standing out from the center of the split pieces that were all that remained of the duke's arrow.

"No." The duke breathed, as if he was too much in awe of

the shot to give the order for my arrest.

I flourished a bow, turning in his direction for the first time. "This has been fun, Duke, but it is time I bid you adieu."

Rather than straightening, I spun and dove into the surrounding crowd.

The courtyard exploded with chaos. The soldiers rushed forward to apprehend me, but they were hampered by the crowd that also surged forward in a tide of shouting, scrambling people. Whether they simply wanted to congratulate their hero or they were trying to protect him, it didn't matter. They provided the distraction I was counting on, though I hoped the soldiers would have enough restraint not to hurt the unarmed villagers.

I darted between soldiers and villagers, hampered by my strung bow gripped in my hand. Two soldiers blocked my way, but instead of slowing, I ducked low and rammed into them with my shoulders. They stumbled aside, and I darted off while they were still regaining their balance.

"Get him!" Duke Guy shouted, his deep voice tinged with frustration.

Sheriff Reinhault appeared before me, brandishing his sword. His mouth tipped in a fierce smile. When I tried to dodge around him, he matched my movements.

I skidded to a halt. I didn't have my own sword, since such weapons would have been confiscated at the castle gate. Nor did I want to use my precious bow for fending off the sheriff.

Instead, I switched my bow to my left hand and took up one of the posts that had been used to outline the edge of one of the cleared areas for the performers. It was heavier than I would have liked, but it was hardened wood with a weighted end on the bottom to keep it upright on the cobblestones.

When the sheriff stabbed with his sword, I parried with the post as a snarl burned in my throat. As thrilling as a swordfight was, I didn't have the time to waste. The duke and his soldiers were closing in behind me. If I didn't disappear soon, all would be lost.

As the sheriff swung again, I ducked, feeling the brush of air against my hair as my hat was partially yanked from my head. It hung down at the back of my head, still obscuring my hair from the duke.

But the sheriff stared straight into my face, part of my braid visible.

Before he could get a good look, I swung the post as hard as I could, the weighted end catching the sheriff's shoulder. He stumbled and fell to his knees, his gaze swinging to the ground rather than focused on me.

I would have to hope his glimpse had been too quick, my eyepatch too concealing, for him to realize just whom he had seen.

I jumped over the sheriff and ran. Dodging a few more grasping hands, I flung open the nearest door into the castle's keep.

Once inside, I raced down the corridor, then ducked into one of the storerooms that connected to the kitchens through a set of back passageways. At the empty kitchens, I threw myself out one of the windows, which had been left open to let in the breeze and cool the air heated by the fires.

As the kitchens were in the base of my tower, I climbed up the stones, glancing over my shoulder occasionally to check for pursuit. But the soldiers hadn't yet managed to follow me, nor were they checking the outside of the castle yet, too focused on keeping the outlaws trapped inside.

As planned, I found my window open. I pulled myself inside, rolling onto the window seat and panting from my long run and climb.

I glanced up to find my six brothers crowding around me, foreheads wrinkling as if they had been worried.

Yanking off my eyepatch, I gave a hearty laugh and sat up, shoving my brothers out of my face. "Now that was quite the lark!"

Will shook his head. "Only you, Robin."

John thumped my back, Tuck gave a few muttered congratulations, and Alan hung back, grinning slightly. But, something still seemed off in their expressions. They should all be celebrating with me, not grinning as if they had something to hide.

I crossed my arms. "All right. Out with it. Please tell me you succeeded in your part of the mission?"

"Not exactly." Alan sighed and plopped onto the floor. Behind him, Munch and Marion seemed to be blocking a pile of something from my view. Alan gestured toward the door. "We found a treasure vault deep below the duke's tower, as you expected. It was filled with piles of gold and jewels and riches you wouldn't believe."

As we had always assumed we would find. Why, then, did my brothers' frowns deepen? I searched their faces, then leaned over, trying to peer past Munch, Marion, and John. "Then what's wrong? Didn't you manage to steal enough to make it worth it?"

"It isn't that." Alan sighed so forcefully that his whole body slumped with his exhale. "Does someone else want to tell her? I certainly don't."

It must be bad news if they were about ready to pick straws to decide who had to tell me. I pushed to my feet, strode across the room, and shoved between the wall of my brothers.

There, in the center of the floor, sat a pile of gold and jewels. Yet, standing this close to them, I could taste the overpowering tang of fae magic coming from the pile. I squinted at it, trying to will away the fae glamor that was lying to my eyes, as I reached down to grip the iron bar in my quiver.

It looked real, but it was fool's gold, nothing more. Fool's gold was a type of faerie gold that the fae used to trick humans. A way to toy with the human vice of greed.

"Ah, now that is an interesting development." I knelt and touched the fool's gold. It rang with the same faint sour taste that I sensed throughout the castle.

None of the duke's gold was real. All this time, I'd believed him fabulously wealthy. Yet, all along, it had been nothing but shiny, worthless bits of fae trickery.

I looked up at my brothers. "Was all the gold in the treasure vaults nothing but an illusion? What if he is substituting fae gold for real gold when he sends the taxes to the king?"

Will shook his head. "Nothing in any of the vaults we searched was real. But, we would have noticed if we robbed a tax shipment and found part of it to be fake. Everything he has been sending to the king has been real."

What was his game? Why, then, have all this fool's gold sitting in his treasure vault? Who was he trying to cheat? I would understand if he was taxing the people for the real money, then sending the fake gold on to the king. But, he wasn't doing that. Instead, the only person he was cheating was himself. And that made no sense whatsoever.

"What are your orders, Robin?" Alan knelt on the floor across from me. Behind him, Will, John, Tuck, Munch, and Marion clustered in closer, waiting to hear what I had to say.

I drew in a deep breath and let it out slowly. "We proceed with the plan. All of you will escape with this fool's gold. I want to know what happens to it when it's taken from the castle, and if the duke notices it's missing. I'll stay here and see if I can get to the bottom of this." I glanced between all of them, taking in their serious faces. "Whatever is going on, it's more than simply a greedy duke trying to get rich off his villagers. A fae is at work here, and it is our job as foresters to stop him."

Chapter Eight

The duke turned the castle inside out looking for the outlaw and his band, searching everywhere except one place. The bedroom of his supposedly resting wife.

And yet, as my brothers wiggled out my window, shimmied down the rope, and vanished into the Greenwood, everything had changed. We had a new mission, but the same enemy.

It was time to prove that Duke Guy was fae and using those powers for some nefarious purpose.

After I rubbed his nose in my victory one more time, of course.

The knock finally came on my door at nearly midnight. I wore a comfortable, loose-fitting dress, as expected of a lady in the throes of suffering.

I took one glance around, checking yet again that no sign of my brothers' presence that day remained in my rooms. Like the other numerous times I'd checked, everything was in order.

I opened the door to find Duke Guy there. He leaned

heavily against the doorjamb, his angular face drawn into deep, weary lines. "I'm sorry to impose at this late hour, my lady. I hope I didn't wake you."

"No, not at all." I kept my voice low and tight, as if I was still recovering. It was an effort to keep my voice soft and empathetic as I said with a straight face, "I heard the outlaw got away. I'm sorry."

During the afternoon, one guard had knocked on my door to ask if the outlaw had come that way. When I'd said no, the soldier had stationed himself at my door to guard me, forcing my brothers to stay very quiet the rest of the day until they had escaped once darkness fell.

The duke's whole body sagged even more against the doorjamb, his dark eyes swinging up to meet mine as if seeking strength or reassurance from me.

I was the last person who could give him those things, but I plastered on a soft look anyway.

He sighed and shook his head. "I'm afraid this means I must leave first thing in the morning to travel to the king's court. He has summoned me to answer for my repeated failures to capture the outlaw, and this latest debacle will not help my case any."

I had to swallow to force my voice into something suitably wifely and sympathetic. "How long will you be gone?"

"A week. Maybe less, if the king has his fill of raking me over the coals quickly." Duke Guy shrugged, his gaze distant as he stared at the ceiling above my head. "Assuming the king allows me to return at all."

I should be hoping that the king removed the duke and solved all my problems. But, I wasn't. The duke was mine to defeat, and it would be a terrible let-down if everything simply ended like that.

The duke's jaw hardened, and his hand shook where it was braced against the jamb. After a long moment of what seemed like internal struggle, he reached under his shirt and pulled out a small key on a chain. His jaw worked as he drew the chain over his head and held out it out to me, the key winking in the candlelight as it swung freely. "While I am gone, please watch over this key for me." He paused, throat constricting. "Do not open the door this key unlocks. Please. If you value your life, do not disobey this command."

As if I would ever obey a command like that. This was the key to the small door that reeked of fae magic. I would finally find out what that door was hiding.

I gave what I hoped was a meek smile as I took the key, gripping it tightly in my hand. "I will take good care of this until you return."

At my words, he squeezed his eyes shut for a moment, almost as if he were in pain.

Yet, when he opened his eyes, his face shuttered, all traces of vulnerability wiped away behind that layer of hard steel. "See that you do. I will ask for it upon my return." He gave a stilted bow. "I will be gone when you awaken, my lady. This is farewell."

Before I could respond, he spun on his heel and strode off at a brisk pace that quickly carried him out of sight.

I uncurled my fingers, revealing the key he'd given me. This too jangled my senses with the whiff of fae magic clinging to it.

Slipping it over my head, I let the key fall inside the dress. Despite the fact that I had been holding it tightly in my hand and it had been resting against the duke's chest, the metal of the key remained strangely cold as it slid against my skin, causing a single shiver to quiver down my back.

Tomorrow night, once the duke was gone, I would investigate that room.

But, for tonight, I had a different plot in mind.

I waited for another few hours, making sure the duke

BLUEBEARD AND THE OUTLAW

would be asleep, before I once again dressed in my Hood costume and slipped out my window.

Yes, I know, it wasn't the smartest thing to wander the castle as the Hood on a night when the castle guards were still alert and watching for me. But I'd had to leave the archery contest before claiming my prize, and I wasn't about to leave it in the duke's hands any longer.

I had to climb out my window to evade the guard outside my door, then I used the servants' passageways to reach the room filled with the stuffed magical beasts. The small door called me, the key warming against my skin, but I pushed past the temptation. Soon, I told the door and the room beyond. Soon.

As before, the stairway to the duke's rooms were guarded, so I had to wriggle out of a window hidden in an alcove and climb up the tower instead. My fingers burned by the time I pulled myself through into the duke's rooms, and I was already dreading the climb back down. My muscles were sore after all the shooting I'd done after a few days with little practice and exercise.

The starlight cast faint light into the duke's room, and I eased from the window seat to the floor, my focus centered on the bed. There, I could just make out the shape of someone sleeping beneath the covers, his breathing deep and even.

The golden arrow lay on a table near the door to the sitting room, bright and winking even in the low light. I tiptoed toward it, pausing to glance at the bed every few seconds.

This could be a trap. The duke could have guessed that the Hood would come for this arrow.

But I had also seen the weariness in him. It had been the despair of a man certain his quarry was well out of his reach. He and his soldiers had searched the castle thoroughly enough that they would have been convinced the outlaw had long vacated its premises.

In that case, the duke would plan to use this arrow to set a trap on the road. After all, he would have to travel through the Greenwood to reach the king. He had to be expecting an ambush then, rather than here in his well-guarded castle.

With my chest tight with the thrill of sneaking through the duke's room, I reached for the golden arrow.

As soon as my fingers brushed it, I knew that this, too, was made of fool's gold rather than the real thing.

No matter. It was my prize, its symbol worth far more to me than whatever material it was made out of.

I slipped the golden arrow into my quiver and drew out one of my black-fletched arrows, setting my arrow where the golden one had lain a moment ago. The duke would know I had been in his room, and he would wake cursing the Hood yet again.

Still, he would also know that I had been in his room and hadn't killed him. That would make him wonder. Perhaps he would realize the Hood had more honor than he had given him credit for. Maybe he would realize the Hood found no pleasure in his death, but only in the chase.

And maybe I didn't know what he would read into my actions, considering I wasn't even sure what I intended by it besides riling him.

I turned to go back to the window, yet halted partway across the room. From this angle, the starlight fell more fully onto the bed, outlining the duke's sleeping form. Even in sleep, his face was craggy with weariness, as if all his guilt pressed upon him even in his attempt to rest.

I crept closer to the bed until I stood over the duke, contemplating him in his repose. From his long nose with that lump from a break to the bare muscles of his shoulders visible above the blanket he held to his chin, it was a strangely intimate glimpse of him. One I should know as his wife, yet it still felt deliciously forbidden.

If I had been in his place, I would have been appalled to discover he had been watching me while I slept. But I pushed that niggling discomfort aside, telling myself that he didn't deserve such niceties after the murders he'd committed.

He rolled onto his back, muttering a few incoherent words, his forehead wrinkling as if he was in pain in his sleep.

I shouldn't have done it. I know I shouldn't have.

But an arrow and a kiss. Those were the prizes of famed archery contests, weren't they? I had claimed the one. It was time to steal the other.

Gently, I brushed my lips against his cheek, then whispered in his ear, "Rest well, Guy, and enjoy pleasant dreams of me."

As I tiptoed across the room and climbed out the window, I couldn't have said which *me* I meant. The Hood. Lady Robin. Or the woman who was somehow both of those and yet neither one.

Chapter Nine

I can hear you shouting at me. Don't open that small door. Don't disobey such a command. It never ends well.

The thing is, I didn't mind if it didn't end well, as long as it wasn't boring.

Besides, ask yourself this. What would you have done in my place? I can guarantee that you would have sought a way to open that door just as I did. It is human nature, after all, to give in to the lure of the forbidden.

I crept through the hall of magical creature mounts, my heart hammering harder with each step I took toward that small door. Finally, I would reveal the mystery that had been haunting me from the day I married the duke.

I'd spent the day waiting in my room, and it had been agony. I'd eaten all my meals up there, avoiding the sheriff. Though, I took the fact that I hadn't been woken by a squad of guards pounding down my door as a sign that either the sheriff hadn't realized who I was or he had refrained from mentioning any suspicions he had to the duke.

As he had said, Duke Guy was long gone by the time for our normal breakfast in the dining room, though I had been up before the sun and had watched him depart, standing at my window overlooking the Greenwood.

I put the white cloth back in my window, signaling my brothers that I was still fine this morning. I also shot an arrow with a note tied to it into the trees, giving strict instructions that my brothers were to let the duke pass through the Greenwood unmolested. It would be no fair if they had all the fun attacking the duke while I wasn't there.

But now, after a day of agonized waiting, the time to open this door was here at last.

I pulled the key on its chain out from underneath my shirt, the key warming even more on my palm as if it, too, was eager for this moment.

I halted in front of the small door, the taste of fae magic so strong on my tongue that I was near choking on it. Gripping the key, I inserted it in the lock and gave myself a single moment to savor the suspense before I turned it.

Unlike the hour I'd spent fruitlessly attempting to pick this lock, the key turned easily and the lock clicked.

I lifted the latch and pushed. The door swung open soundlessly. Perhaps too soundlessly.

Pitch darkness waited beyond, telling me that this room lacked a window to let in even a hint of starlight. I had a candle, flint, and striker tucked into a pocket, but I couldn't light it until I was inside the room with the door closed behind me to prevent the guards seeing the light.

I took a long, purposeful step into the room. Fae magic washed over me, so thick it was almost a tangible thing. After taking the key from the lock, I eased the door shut behind me.

Lights blazed to life, so sharp and bright I stifled a cry and shut my eyes against the glare.

I smelled blood. A stench of iron and rot and death.

After a moment, I squinted, trying to make out something of the room through my lashes. The first thing I saw was a flood of deep red covering the floor and flowing up onto the wall. Above the tide of red, three figures in white dangled against the stone.

My eyes flew open, and I stared at the sight before me.

Three dead women hung from ropes, blood staining their white nightgowns and drooling down their bodies to form a pool on the floor. Their faces were the blue-gray of death while each one had blonde hair, as I did.

The key slipped from my fingers and landed in the puddle of blood with a faint plink.

Blast and bother, *what* was going on here?

Yet, the longer I stood there staring, the more I saw the flaws. I was a forester, even before I was an outlaw. I had seen plenty of dead animals, both ones I had killed and those who had died and were decomposing. I knew death's look. Its reek. Its decay.

And this sight before me was definitely not it.

The duke's first wife had been dead for nearly eight years while the second wife had been dead five years and the last two years. After that long, they shouldn't have looked this pristine. The blood shouldn't have smelled fresh and newly spilled, but instead would have been dried and rotted. All of this illusion before me had been put together for shock value, not accuracy.

I squeezed my eyes shut again and focused on my honed senses. Eyes were easily fooled by fae magic, and the fae magic would use the eyes to help trick the other senses. If you saw blood, the magic would make you smell it since that was what your mind was expecting. If you beheld a dead body, the fae magic would make it real enough to touch since your eyesight was telling you it was there.

But with my eyes closed, I could sort through what was real and what was a glamor, though it would have been easier if I hadn't left my quiver with its iron rod in the hiding spot in my room.

Yes, I smelled blood. But I could now tell the odor was attempting to disguise the fae magic's normal overpowering sweetness.

When I took a step forward, my boots scuffed on bare stone floor rather than squish in something wet and sticky. When I reached out a hand, my fingers found a bare stone wall rather than the cold stiffness of a dead body.

Keeping my eyes closed, I explored along the wall by feel. For several yards, my hands touched nothing but stone. Then, I bumped into something that swung away from me. My heart leapt into my throat, a good and proper jolt.

But fear was so utterly thrilling. I would have been terribly disappointed if this room had been empty of everything but gory fae illusions.

Stilling, I ran my fingers over the rough thing I'd bumped into. Tightly twisted sisal fibers scratched against my hand. It was a rope. A thick rope with…

Now I swallowed, my stomach giving a flip that wasn't quite as pleasant as before.

This was a noose. A very real, very empty noose just waiting for the duke's fourth wife.

Waiting for me.

I straightened my shoulders and opened my eyes, staring at the empty noose swinging gently against the wall before me. The rope ran up to a pulley attached to the ceiling before going back down to a ring on the next wall where the other end had been tied.

I glanced once more around the room. My inner senses

had cut through the fae magic enough that I could now see that this noose was the only thing here.

This was a room designed for murder.

Still, a noose was nothing to get all squinchy about. I'd been dancing around a hanging ever since I took on the role of the Hood. So what if I danced a little closer to it by being the duke's wife? He couldn't hang me twice.

But I couldn't fully banish the shadowy shiver of knowing that, even if those bodies had been a fae illusions, their deaths were all too real. Those three women had been killed in this room. Probably hung from a rope in this very spot.

Yet the illusions had shown me not just the dead women hanging, but also blood, which wouldn't have been spilled if their deaths had been only by hanging.

Was that merely a part of the fae illusion, put in for the added gore? Or did the glamor hold a shred of truth, showing a past that had occurred in this room? What kind of gruesome murder had those women endured?

I'd known the duke was cruel. I'd known he'd killed his three wives. But this was sadistic in a way I hadn't anticipated. This was murder done as if it was enjoyable.

My head was tearing in two, as I tried to imagine the man who had so gently cradled a squirming, terrified dog then turning around and taking pleasure in committing a murder such as this not once, but three times.

Perhaps it was possible. Maybe a man could love a pet and yet kill in the most gruesome fashion possible.

Or there was something else going on here. Something beyond mere murder, horrible as it was.

I had seen all there was to see here. No sense in lingering in this place.

I turned and marched to the door, forcing my steps to remain even and brisk. At the door, I halted and bent to pick up the key I'd dropped on the floor.

Even though the rest of the illusions had faded, the key was still covered with red splotches, as if stained with blood. I rubbed at the stains, but they didn't come off. Nor did I feel anything on the key, whether with my eyes open or closed.

The bodies and the blood had been glamor. But this was something else entirely. The stains were a part of the metal of the key itself in a way that made me think this key was wrapped up in the enchantment in a way the illusions had not.

What was the goal of all of this? What did the duke hope to gain with all the trickery and horrific illusions and murders?

He might be just that evil. That was all there was to it.

And that made it rather uncomfortable that I was attracted to him. Sure, I was drawn to danger. I enjoyed tasting a dose of fear now and again.

But being actively, knowingly attracted to someone capable of this level of depravity? That was something else entirely.

With another shiver, I slid the chain over my head once again, tucking the bloodstained key out of sight beneath my shirt.

Suddenly, this game I played with the duke wasn't that fun anymore.

THE NEXT MORNING, I forced myself to walk to the dining room for breakfast as if everything was normal. It was time I faced the sheriff, even if my skin was crawling with all the danger and fae magic drenching this place. The duke might be gone visiting the king, but his menace still cloaked this castle.

I had to get a hold of myself and find my swagger again. I

didn't like this jumpy, shaken person I'd turned into overnight.

I wore a deep blue velvet dress that someone had done a good job of lengthening by adding six inches of lace and ribbons at the hem.

The dress must have belonged to one of the duke's previous wives, and as I put on the poor dead woman's dress, I silently promised the long-dead woman that I would avenge her by killing her killer. The injustice of her death would not linger.

When I pushed open the doors to the dining room, I found Sheriff Reinhault already there, seated in his usual place to the duke's right. As I entered, the sheriff hopped to his feet, and he gave me a broad smile when I approached my chair. "You are lovely this morning, Your Grace. Though, I have heard that you are unwell?"

"It is nothing. I am much improved today." I waved one hand as I took my seat across from Sheriff Reinhault.

As Sheriff Reinhault reclaimed his seat, he studied me for a long moment. "You and the duke seem to be getting on better than before."

What was I supposed to say to that? I gave a slight shrug. I couldn't show the way my skin prickled with the memory of those fae illusions. "He was kind to the villagers during the flood. Perhaps there is more to him than there seems."

There was definitely more, all right. There was the side of him that hung his wives, then took twisted pleasure in carving them up afterwards.

Even I didn't dare voice that out loud to the duke's loyal minion. Perhaps I would, once I got my fortitude back. But not this morning.

"All of us are more than we seem." The sheriff's mouth twisted, his light blue eyes flashing with something. Maybe humor, but with a hint of bitter darkness to it. "Don't be fooled by the duke, milady. It would be a pity if you were killed like the others. He placed the rope around their necks with his own hands, you know."

I stiffened, that shadowy shiver returning to my back. The sheriff had to have been there when the duke did the deed. He would have seen the atrocities that had occurred behind that locked door.

And yet, he said the words as if he knew that I had seen more than I should have. As if he knew I had trespassed in that room.

He couldn't possibly know. I had been careful. No one had seen me.

I was just being paranoid, brought on by what I'd seen last night and my worries of what the sheriff might have seen during my getaway from the archery contest.

It was common knowledge that the duke had hung his wives. That was how the duke had gotten away with it all this time, by claiming their murders had been suicide. That was what the sheriff was referencing, not my particular knowledge of how the deed was done.

I gathered my wits. This was not the time to fall apart. I was the Hood. An outlaw. I had faced danger many times. I was supposed to be enjoying this little scheme of mine, not quaking in my boots.

"You witnessed his murder of his previous wives? And you haven't reported this to the king?" I leaned my elbows on the table, piercing the sheriff with a stare.

"It is my word against the duke's. Who do you think the king would believe?" Sheriff Reinhault shrugged. "Instead, I must stay where I can attempt to do the most good."

I understood that. I stayed and did my best, though I couldn't seem to change things no matter how hard I tried.

My entire plan had fallen apart. There was no gold for me to steal. Every coin, jewel, and scrap of metal in the duke's vault was utterly worthless fool's gold. I had nothing to give the villagers. No way to lower the taxes. No means to prove the duke's guilt in a way the king would believe any more than the sheriff did.

And, most of all, I had no idea how to banish the ache in my chest at the thought of killing the duke.

Sheriff Reinhault leaned forward, his blue eyes sympathetic, his face open. "If you need help, you can come to me, Lady Robin."

I managed a nod, though I didn't speak.

Was this why he hadn't reported any suspicions about me to the duke? Could he perhaps be an ally?

Yet, some instinct warned me to be silent. And so I was, as we ate our breakfast and the sheriff left the room to see to his duties.

Could I even trust my instincts anymore? Those instincts kept tugging to trust the duke, after all. My head and my heart were all too messed up at the moment to think clearly.

Too bad this was when I needed a clear head the most.

Chapter Ten

I know I should have told my brothers about the room and the illusion of blood and dead bodies. But a part of me didn't want to tell it and admit to even a momentary feeling of true fear.

Besides, they might have done something foolish if they knew. This was my fight. I was determined to see it through to the end, no matter what that end might be.

I had the white cloth in the window. I would be fine.

Probably.

As I strode toward the dining hall on the fifth evening after the duke had left, the sound of bootsteps pounding on the carpet hurried in my direction.

I halted, wishing I had more than the small knife tucked into my belt. My instincts were prickling, the swell of fae magic in this castle building to a level I'd not yet sensed.

Whatever plot or power had been simmering here was about to be unleashed.

Duke Guy sprinted around the corner. As soon as his gaze landed on me, he raced to me and gripped my upper arms before I could do more than take a step backward to put my back to the wall. His dark eyes focused on me, more frantic and pained than I'd ever seen. "Please tell me you didn't open that door. Please."

It was odd, his pleading. He should have returned with demands to see the key, not this panicked begging.

I didn't like to see this strong, cold man in this state. He was a man for witty banter and hardened resolve to uphold the law. Not...this.

Still, I felt my mouth quirk as I pulled the chain and key from underneath the bodice of my dress. "I hate to disappoint you, but it seems that I did."

The key swung between us, winking gold and red in the candlelight.

Duke Guy's shoulders slumped, his hands quivering against my arms. "Then, Robin, if you listen to nothing else I've said, listen to this. Run. Get out of this castle. Flee as far and as fast as you can."

"Come now, human. You know that isn't how this works." Sheriff Reinhault's voice rang down the corridor from behind Duke Guy.

Except, that it wasn't the sheriff's voice. Not exactly. The good-humored cheeriness remained, but it was now layered with something darker and sleeker.

Duke Guy slumped farther, his shoulders shaking now as well as his hands, his grip going slack on my arms.

I slid along the wall out of his grasp, giving myself space to run if I needed it.

Sheriff Reinhault slunk down the corridor toward us, a self-satisfied smirk on a face that seemed even more otherworldly beautiful than before. Instead of his usual queue, his blond hair was down so that it trailed over his shoulders. But most disturbing of all were the points of his tapered ears that showed between strands of his hair, no longer covered as they had been before.

He was a fae. The sheriff, not the duke, was the fae my brothers and I had been hunting ever since we'd stumbled across the fae magic here at the castle.

Where were the guards? The servants? The castle had gone deathly still around us, suffocating with powerful fae magic.

Reinhault was no half-fae or quarter-fae. He was a full fae with the power to toy with us however he wished, even with the restrictions of no lying and burning iron that full fae experienced here in the human world.

Not that he seemed all that restricted. He was wearing a sword at his hip, which should have been too much iron for him to handle.

That could only mean one thing...something truly terrifying that my forester parents had taught me years ago about the fae.

Blast. I was in trouble. And not the fun kind of trouble either.

Duke Guy's eyes shot to mine. "Run," he whispered before he whirled and threw himself at Reinhault.

This time, I listened. I spun and raced down the passageway, stretching my long legs with every stride. Fae magic burst through my senses, but I kept running. I didn't bother trying the door to the outside, knowing it would be locked tight against me the way the small door had been.

Instead, I raced up the tower until I reached my bedroom. I skidded inside, barring the outer door, and darted across the sitting room into the bedchamber. I locked that door too before I raced to the window. I tossed the pillows from the bench, then yanked the wooden bench top off, letting it crash to the floor with a clunk.

Inside lay my sword, quiver, and unstrung bow. I fumbled to buckle on the quiver and sword before I shrugged into the sheath that held my bow across my back.

A crash of splintering wood came from the outer room.

I furiously cranked the window open, letting in a blast of evening air. The white cloth fluttered as it fell free, tumbling out the window and flapping on its way to the ground far below.

The door to my room exploded inward, shooting shards of wood and debris in all directions. They stung my arms and back as I lunged out the window, scrambling for the now-familiar toe and hand holds.

A firm hand dug into the back of my bodice and yanked me back inside. I tumbled over the window seat and came up hard against Duke Guy's chest.

His grip was iron as he spun me, holding both of my arms pinned behind my back. Yet, the glimpse I had of his eyes held a frantic pain.

Reinhault's mouth curled as he stepped over the remains of the door. "A good attempt, milady, but not good enough. You sealed your fate the moment you disobeyed your husband and turned that key in the lock."

"It was not...an order...I wanted to give." Duke Guy's voice came out strained and shaking, his breath hot against the back of my neck. "Please. Let her go. Let this one go."

I squirmed, trying to yank free of the duke's hold. Despite his pleading, his hold on my arms remained solid and unbreakable.

Not his hold. The fae's. However it happened, this fae Reinhault had control of the duke's actions, even if his mind remained his own.

"You know I can't do that. I need her blood, as I did the others." Reinhault's mouth quirked, his blue eyes flashing with yet more amusement. "Besides, this wife of yours has been particularly naughty. I would think you would want to see her hang. You've sought just that, often enough."

I stilled. Sheriff Reinhault had put it together. He'd realized exactly who I was after that glimpse he'd gotten at the archery tournament.

"What does he mean?" Guy's question was a breath in my ear.

"Do you want to tell him, or should I?" Reinhault gave a slithering smirk before he continued, not giving me a chance to answer. "Your wife, Duke Guy, is the infamous outlaw known as the Hood."

Well, no going back now. I drew myself together and glanced over my shoulder at him, meeting his wide, dark gray-brown eyes. I deepened my voice to the one he'd heard so many times as I taunted him. "Hello, Duke Bluebeard, it seems you have caught me at last."

He closed his eyes, his face twisting as if I'd shot him with those words.

"As you can see, this one actually deserves the rope you'll put around her neck." Reinhault shouldn't have sounded so smugly satisfied. He gestured toward the door. "I'm just giving you what you've wanted for years. A chance to hang the Hood."

Duke Guy's fingers tightened on my arms to the point of bruising, and he took one jolting step, then two, bodily hauling me toward the door.

I dug in my heels, but even with my height and strength, I was no match for his yet taller, stronger frame, especially under fae power as he was right now.

My brothers would be coming. I had to believe that. It didn't matter that it was nearly dusk and it would be easy to rationalize the white cloth coming down as merely my normal routine.

One of my brothers would have been watching the castle.

He would have seen the white cloth fall out the window to the ground and my attempt to escape. He would recognize my call for help.

Yet, they wouldn't get here in time. They had to come up with a plan, storm this castle locked up tight with fae magic, and somehow find their way to where I was in the castle.

I was shoved inexorably down the stairs and through the corridors toward that room of horrors locked behind the small door.

As we halted in front of the door, Reinhault turned to me, his lips parting as he stepped closer to me. He leaned in, trailing a finger down my neck until he hooked it under the chain holding the small key. "I'll be taking this now." He gave a sharp yank on the chain, and it broke with a painful snap at the back of my neck.

He rubbed his thumb over the key, as if relishing the bloodstains swirling across the glowing metal. "You just couldn't resist. They never do."

I gritted my teeth and didn't respond. I needed to focus my wits on escaping rather than on a retort.

"No comment? I'm disappointed in you." Reinhault shook his head as he turned the key in the lock. "I would think you'd want to make full use of that voice of yours, before I silence it."

The fact that he wanted me to speak only made me more determined to keep my mouth shut.

As Guy hauled me into the room in Reinhault's footsteps, I took stock of what I had.

I had my knife and my sword, though I couldn't draw either one with my hands pinned by Guy's merciless grip. I had my arrows, but they would do me little good while my bow was still unstrung and sheathed across my back.

While Reinhault halted by the door, Guy brushed past him, shoving me in front of him until we reached the wall holding the single, empty noose. None of the illusions of dead bodies and blood were visible, but they didn't need to be. Not now when that noose was so stark against the stone, waiting there for me.

Duke Guy pressed me to the wall, one hand gripping both of my wrists while, with the other, he slid the noose over my head. The fibers chafed against my neck, cruel and taunting.

The duke paused, his agonized gaze swung to mine for a brief, heartfelt moment. "I'm so sorry. I—" Whatever he had been about to say choked off, and he reeled a step backwards as if yanked by an invisible hand.

As soon as he released my hands, I reached up, gripped the noose, and tried to pull it off.

It refused to budge. Even though it was clearly loose enough to slip off my head, it wouldn't lift that high, no matter how hard I strained.

Reinhault made a tutting sound as he softly clicked the door shut. "You are a forester's daughter. I would think you of all people should know how this works. By marrying him, you are as bound to his bargain as he is."

In other words, it was fae magic keeping that noose around my neck. I had no hope of pulling it off.

Especially if the magic was originally tied to the duke, and not to me. I had my iron rod stuffed in my quiver, but even if I gripped it, it likely wouldn't be enough to stave off this magic. I would need the duke to hold iron, and he was now out of my reach, marching across the room with stilted strides.

Guy halted at the ring set in the wall and took up the end of the rope, gripping it with white knuckles.

My stomach lurched. This was no sudden drop and a broken neck kind of hanging, one that was over quickly. No, this was a hoist-me-off-my-feet-and-let-me-choke-long-and-slow type of hanging. Unpleasant and gruesome.

I dropped my hands from the noose and, even though the duke was the one holding the rope, I faced Reinhault, the one who truly had my life in his hands. I had to keep him talking and distracted. That was my only chance to buy myself enough time.

Reaching behind me, I gave the fae my most infuriating smirk. "And what is this bargain? Surely I deserve to know, since it seems my life is forfeit because of it."

Reinhault's gaze swept over me languidly, as if he was reveling in the sight of me wearing that noose around my neck. "A simple bargain. All the wealth and luxuries he could imagine, as long as his wife was obedient. He should have known better than make a bargain like that."

How I wanted to put an arrow through this monster's eye. I kept my smirk in place as I fumbled with the ties holding my unstrung bow in place, trying to keep my shoulders as still as possible to hide what I was doing. "That does sound like a pretty foolish bargain to make."

"Yes, but he was greedy. So was his wife. Human nature makes you such pathetic creatures to toy with." Reinhault shook his head, almost as if he truly had compassion for me. "Even as each of his wives stood there, the noose around their necks, they could never let go of the longing for wealth and treasure. And you, Robin of the Greenwood, are the worst of the lot. You are consumed with thoughts of gold and how you might steal it. If that rope remains around your neck, it is because you covet the wealth I provide."

I wasn't greedy, was I? I didn't want gold for myself. Only for the hurting villagers.

But that noose was still around my neck, and I didn't know if it was because of the fae's power or my traitorous heart.

Out of the corner of my eye, I could see Duke Guy's black

hair, his head bent as if he couldn't bear to watch this take place yet again.

My bow came free, sliding down my back and into my hands. I eased one end to the floor and braced it in the corner where wall met floor. Straining with my arms twisted behind my back, I had all the wrong angles for bending the bow and slipping the string up and into place.

But I had to try.

"By the way," I kept my voice free of any sign of strain as I wrestled with my bow behind my back. "How do you know who I am? I know how you figured I am the Hood, but how do you know I am the daughter of foresters?"

"There was always something familiar about your face." Reinhault's jaw flexed, but then the expression smoothed into that smarmy sadistic one once again. "You have your mother's hair. Your father's stubborn chin. I should have put it together sooner, but human faces do look so terribly distorted when they are lying dead and mutilated on the forest floor."

I froze, my bowstring only a fraction away from slipping into its notch at the end of the bow's arm.

Reinhault had killed my parents. He was the monster who had come through the faerie circle that day. The one evil creature my parents had failed to stop.

He had more blood on his hands than I'd thought. My head spun with all that had happened in the past ten years.

If Reinhault had killed my parents, then he'd likely also killed the duke's parents, who had died only a year after mine. I'd already realized that he was the true killer of the duke's three wives, even if he'd maliciously forced the duke to pull the rope himself.

It was beyond time for this fae to meet justice. And I was a forester, tasked with dealing such justice on the fae and their monsters who dared venture into my forest. No wonder Reinhault must have forced Guy to disband the foresters. We were the only ones with the knowledge to stop him.

Reinhault must have seen something in my eyes, for he gestured to Duke Guy. "Enough. I have granted your last wish and answered your questions. Now it is time to give this outlaw her just reward."

The string of my bow slid into place and held, even as the noose tightened around my neck.

My breath seized, stars bursting across my eyes, as I was hoisted off my feet, my back scraping against the wall.

Even as my instincts screamed that I needed to claw at the thing cutting into my neck and shooting agony into my head, I forced my hand to drop to my quiver and trail along my arrows, finding the one I wanted by feel and by that resonating call inside my chest.

I would have the strength and will for one shot only. I braced my boots against the wall at my back, trying to twist my body into something of a proper stance. As I nocked the arrow, my blood roared in my ears, warning me of the death that was creeping toward me with every second I dangled from that rope.

"Now this is a new game. What are you going to do, little archer?" Reinhault's face was a wavering blur among the encroaching black. "You have to know his bargain doesn't allow you to kill me. Otherwise he would have done so long ago."

Yet as I drew the bow back, my back and arms straining, the arrow's gleaming iron tip pointed at Duke Guy's chest instead of Reinhault.

As if sensing the impending danger, Duke Guy looked up. His gaze met mine, and at that moment I wasn't sure if his gaze or mine was the more pained.

"Kill me." It sounded like little more than a whisper,

though he must have spoken it far louder than that for me to hear over the pounding in my ears. Even through the fae's control, he gave a shudder. "Kill me and save yourself."

"Oh, yes." Reinhault's voice was almost a purr, smooth and sultry. "Kill him. You've wanted to do it for years. You are going to die. You should have the satisfaction of taking your greatest enemy down with you."

The arrow's white fletching tickled my cheek as I reached full draw, my elbow knocking against the stone wall behind me.

It was down to me, the arrow, my target. I had no breath to release in a steadying exhale. No instant to hesitate or my arm would waver.

Slowly, deliberately, I released the arrow.

Chapter Eleven

When I was ten, I spent many hours sitting at my father's feet while he fletched arrow after arrow and instructed me on the ways of foresters and fae.

"The fae are strong, but our world weakens them. It binds them with the inability to lie and burns them with our iron." My father never glanced up from his work, his hands always sure and strong and gentle. "But you must be wary. There are two ways a fae can evade these bindings."

I leaned forward, my hands stilling on the child-sized bow I cradled in my lap. "How?"

"The first is through marriage to a human, though the human must enter into the union willingly. Many a fae has stolen away a bride, only to find his bride's unwillingness denies him what he seeks." If my father worried about telling such things to a ten-year-old, his face never showed it.

But I was a forester's daughter, and I already knew that it was my duty to stand in the place between fae and human, their realm and ours, and guard it with my bow, my sword, and my life if necessary. "And the other?"

My father tied off the fletching, spinning the arrow in his fingers a moment before he looked at me. "The fae must spill a human's blood in a deed so dark, so despicable, that the fae themselves will not speak of it. They will cast out their own kind who perform such things. Nor will that fae stop at one death. He will find he needs to kill again and again to keep the blood's protection."

I gave a shudder, the day seeming more shadowed than before. "Ick."

My father placed his newly finished arrow in my hand, curling my fingers around it. "If you ever meet such a fae, little bird, then you must take up your bow and hope with all the breath in your body that your arrow flies straight and strikes true."

Due to my horrible stance, dangling as I was, the bowstring slapped the inside of my left arm, stinging, though I had no breath to cry out.

The arrow sliced the magic-laden air and thudded into my target.

Duke Guy staggered from the impact of the arrow to his shoulder. He fell, the rope sliding from his fingers.

I dropped to the floor, gagging and staggering. I braced myself against the wall and managed to keep my feet beneath me, even as the room seemed to tilt. My chest was convulsing, blackness tunneling my vision.

But as I forced myself straighter, I came up with a second arrow in my hand. This time it was black fletching that tucked against my fingers as I nocked the arrow.

For the first time, Reinhault's eyes widened, and he backed up a step. I had put iron into Duke Guy, deep into his blood and muscle, and now the fae magic of the bargain had been weakened. It would be a momentary weakness, but it was one I could exploit.

The fae held up his hands, as if he was prepared to beg.

"No. No, you can't kill me. If you do, all the wealth of this castle will disappear. And the monsters. Haven't you wondered why there has been a lack of monster attacks in the past ten years? That has been my doing. They will come back if I'm killed, worse than ever. You don't know what has been going on in the Fae Realm. Monsters have been pouring into there, and they will flood into here too if I'm not there to stop them."

With my feet under me, I adjusted my stance, the bow wavering in my fading grip as I struggled to draw it back.

Reinhault backed up another step, fumbling behind him for the latch to the door. "And the weather. I caused the drought, and now that I've messed with your weather, everything is off balance. You'll experience storms like you've never imagined. You need me. Bargain with me. I can give you gold. Riches. Anything your heart desires."

I didn't want gold or riches. If fae monsters came, we would handle them. Same with storms.

The broadhead lifted, the bow bending to the last of my strength. Forget splitting the duke's arrow. This shot—with my vision black, my strength gone, my breath snuffed—was the impossible one.

Fly straight, I willed the arrow. *Strike true.*

I released.

The arrow hissed away, but I couldn't see it. I let myself fall into the darkness, my bow slipping from my fingers.

Across the room there was a meaty thunk. A cry. A thud of a body hitting the ground.

Then I was on the stone floor, wracked with shudders. Perhaps it was me convulsing. Maybe it was the whole castle quaking and falling apart around me.

Guy's deep voice shouted something far too close to my ear, and yet too distant for me to hear. Fingers clawed at the rope, and it took me a moment to process that they weren't mine. I feebly fumbled to help, though I likely did nothing but get in the way.

The constriction eased, but for a moment, I couldn't seem to get my lungs to function, my throat to open. It was as if my body, so long denied air, had forgotten how to breathe.

A heavy hand thumped my back, and I coughed, gagging and choking as the bile in my stomach threatened to come up even as I tried to gulp air down.

The noose was lifted over my head, then an arm wrapped around my shoulders, pulling me into a sitting position crushed against a firm, warm chest.

"You're alive." Duke Guy murmured, his shoulder shaking beneath me. With what emotion, exactly, I couldn't have said. Fear or horror or relief. Maybe all of them. He murmured something more, but it was unintelligible as he pressed his face against my hair and gripped me tightly enough his arm dug into my spine.

If the last few moments had been terrible for me, they had been just as bad for him as he was unwillingly forced to hoist the rope himself. What torments had this man suffered these past years, trapped in a bargain with that sadistic fae and forced to commit unspeakable murders? How had he held himself together under the weight of the guilt of watching his hands perform the awful deeds again and again, even if it hadn't been by his will?

All these years, I'd painted Duke Guy in the role of the villain when all along he'd been the hero, trapped by the true villain.

I wasn't sure what that made me. The Hood wasn't the hero, as I'd always believed. Neither was I the villain. In the end, I was the nuisance, low-level antagonist that made the hero's life harder during his struggle with the story's real villain.

Shakily, still gasping in lungfuls of precious air, I peeled my eyes open and pushed away from him, my left hand squishing in something warm and wet soaking the front of his shirt.

I glanced down to see the arrow I'd put in him still sticking out the upper right side of his chest. The wound bled, but the blood wasn't spurting. I had missed the major blood vessels in his shoulder, as I had aimed to do.

The shaft bumped against my shoulder as I moved, and he sucked in a pained breath.

His arms eased from around me, as if he had just realized what he was doing. His gaze flicked up to mine before dropping. "I am sorry. So sorry."

I wasn't sure if he was apologizing for the almost hanging or the hug afterwards. Probably both. I had to swallow several times, pain shooting up my throat. When I spoke, my voice croaked and tears pricked my eyes with the ache. "Not your fault."

Guy lifted his hand, his fingers coming close to brushing my neck and the bruises there. But he stopped short of touching me, dropping his hand after a long, strained moment. "We should summon the physician. You're injured."

"As are you." Since I had no such compunction against touching him, I pressed a hand to his wound, warm blood dribbling between my fingers.

He gave a grunt, glancing down at my hand and the arrow still sticking from him. He shuddered as the tension left his shoulders, and when he spoke, it sounded much more like the Duke Guy who chased the Hood through the forest for so many years. "You shot me. You actually shot me."

I pushed through the rasping pain in my throat and grinned. "You know I've wanted to do that for a long time. It is so satisfying to finally accomplish one of my goals in life."

Guy's deep eyes lifted to mine once again, not looking away this time. "And yet you didn't kill me, and you've wanted to do that for a long time as well. Should I assume I'm alive because your shot went astray?"

I huffed and pressed my hand harder against the wound. "I put this arrow exactly where I wanted it. Just like I did that one."

With my free hand, I gestured toward Reinhault's body, my arrow buried so deeply in his heart that only the fletching was visible as it pierced through him.

Guy glanced in that direction, and he gave another, smaller shake. "I suppose I should be grateful that I find myself married to an outlaw."

After all we'd been through in the past few minutes, I shouldn't let that jab sting. He had a right to be hurt, after finding out his wife had deceived him and was secretly the outlaw he'd been hunting for years.

"Yes, you should. You should also be grateful I used a tiny little practice arrow on you." Unlike the large, barbed and deadly broadhead I'd put into Reinhault. "I had to get iron into you somehow, and it will pull out easily enough, once the physician has a chance to look at you."

He gave that noncommittal grunt and made no move to stand.

I wanted to stand and haul him to his feet after me, but I was still too shaky myself.

Bootsteps pounded outside the door a moment before it was flung open, slamming into Reinhault's body hard enough to make it flop against the floor.

Will skidded to a halt, nearly tripping on the dead fae sprawled across the threshold. John, Tuck, Alan, Munch, and Marion crowded in behind him, all of them armed to the teeth and carrying death in their eyes.

Will's gaze shot from the dead Reinhault up to me, his gaze focusing on my neck. His jaw hardened, eyes flashing as he drew his sword. "Get away from her, Bluebeard."

"Will." I croaked his name as I scrambled on my hands and knees to place myself between Guy and my avenging brothers. "Don't hurt him."

"He nearly killed you." Will raised his sword, such murder in his face that I hardly knew my own brother.

I glanced past him to the others, but by the steel in their expressions, I knew they were all with Will on this.

I planted a hand on Guy's shoulder and leveraged to my feet, swaying. When he moved to stand as well, I leaned harder on his shoulder, keeping him kneeling on the ground where he would look less threatening to my brothers. The pressure must have communicated more than simply an order to stay on the ground because Guy remained silent, making no attempt to defend himself.

With as deep a breath as I could manage, I rasped out, "This isn't what you think. It isn't what any of us thought. Duke Guy didn't kill his wives. Reinhault did."

That brought Will up so short that John ran into his back, causing Will to stumble a step before he regained his balance. When he straightened, Will searched my face. "Are you sure?"

Guy's tortured guilt might argue with me on that, but he couldn't be held responsible for something he was forced to do against his will. Yes, I still had a few questions, and I would have those out with Guy later.

For now, I pointed at my neck. "Yeah, pretty dead sure. Reinhault is the one responsible for all of this. Look at him. He's *fae*."

"What?" Will spun, but Munch, being the last one into the room, was the first to nudge Reinhault's head with a boot, tipping it so that the hair parted and the tapered ear was visible.

Several of my brothers swore, before they glanced at me and snapped their mouths shut.

It was time to take charge of the situation. I could tell

them the rest later. Such as how it had been Reinhault who had killed our parents and started this drought. Right now, we had more important things to deal with.

"John, Tuck, and Alan, take charge of Reinhault's body. Don't let it out of your sight. And I mean not even for a second. Cut off his head for good measure. I want to be absolutely sure he is dead and stays dead." I finally relaxed my grip on the duke's shoulder, taking a step forward to better boss around my brothers. "Munch and Marion, start getting a pyre ready in the main courtyard. If anyone gives you any trouble, tell them Lady Robin gave the order. If they still give you trouble, send them to me."

The five of them nodded and straightened as they took my orders.

This was my merry band, and it ached inside me that this would likely be the last time we truly operated as an outlaw crew. After today, everything would change.

When I glanced over my shoulder, Duke Guy was still kneeling on the floor, a hand pressed to his wound, his fingers splayed around the arrow shaft. He hunched now, as if the pain of the arrow I'd put in him was finally catching up after the rush of a moment before.

Yes, everything would change. But that change would be for the better.

Will knelt, picked up my bow, and held it out to me. His gaze flicked from me to Guy and back before he exhaled a long sigh. "Really, Robin? Him?"

I took the bow, the wood smooth and familiar against my fingers. Yes, it was strange that, when I found myself attracted to a man, it would be my nemesis. "Yep, him."

Will huffed out another sigh, shaking his head. "Fine. Then I'll help you get him to the physician."

Chapter Twelve

And now we come to it. The explanation of everything. I know it is a long stretch of lots of talking, and I consider it the boring part. But I suppose it is rather important. You might find it interesting, if nothing else.

We stood around the crackling pyre as it consumed Reinhault's body. We might have looked like a solemn group of mourners, if not for my brothers gleefully tossing more wood on the fire to make sure it burned hot and bright and devouring.

The acrid smoke tore at my aching throat, but I remained where I was, standing between Guy and Will. I wanted to watch Reinhault's body vanish into smoke and ash, making certain the fae was well and truly gone for good.

The rest of my brothers formed a half circle around the pyre, leaving a wide space on the other side of Guy from me. I might have vouched for him, but my brothers weren't about to welcome him to the pack with back slaps and brother hugs just yet.

Not that I blamed them. I wasn't sure where I stood with the duke yet either. He'd emerged from the physician's ministrations with a bandage over his wound, his arm in a sling, and a hollow, worn look to his eyes. Even now, he stared at the fire with unblinking focus, his face blank.

The physician had given me a balm for my neck, but I had refused the bandage. I wasn't ready to endure something so constricting around my throat just yet.

Besides, let everyone see the bruises and torn skin. Let them see that I was the wife who survived.

The castle's servants and soldiers gathered in a larger ring around our small group, also solemn and perhaps a bit confused. Duke Guy had said very little to them about how and why Sheriff Reinhault was now dead and getting burned rather than buried. The only explanation I had given for my bruised and torn neck was that Reinhault did it.

Nor had anyone directly asked about the sudden state of the castle. In moments it had gone from the picture of luxury to a run-down thing badly in need of repairs. Its interior was now decorated with shabby carpets and brass fixtures where there once had been gold.

When the fire finally burned low and the stars were high and bright in the nighttime sky overhead, the duke shook off his ruminations and turned to me, though he didn't hold out his arm. "Would you walk with me, my lady?"

Was it a good sign or a bad one that he was still calling me his lady?

As I fell into step with the duke, I shot a glance over my shoulder to give my brothers a warning glare to stay put and not follow.

Alan rolled his eyes, but they remained quiet and where they were.

The duke strode in the direction of the outer wall, the soldiers parting before us with slight bows before they hurried away into the darkness.

When we had climbed the steps and found a section of the wall top that remained good and sturdy, I leaned against the battlements. "You know I'm not really a lady."

"As long as you are married to me, you are a lady, regardless of your previous station or lack thereof." The duke rested his elbows on the stone, staring off into the night rather than at me. "You claimed to be a lady from Loxsley. Is Robin even your real name? If you used a false name at our wedding, then our marriage isn't legal."

This conversation was going to be so boring if he was going to be this serious the whole time. I boosted myself onto the wall top so that I was sitting with my back to the dark countryside and facing Guy. Torches blazed along the wall top every few yards, flicking orange light across his face. I grinned down at him. "I hate to break it to you, Duke Guy, but our marriage is definitely legal. The only thing I lied about is my age. I'm really twenty-nine, not twenty-four."

"Then I will stop feeling uncomfortable at the nearly ten-year age gap." Guy heaved a sigh, staring at the dark blur of the forest.

I knew I had begun to like this man. His reaction to my true age just confirmed my instincts. "I might have left out a few things, but I didn't lie about anything else. I had to make sure I legally inherited everything after I killed you, so I used only my real name Robin in both the vows and on the wedding certificate."

He gave something like a bitter laugh, his head hanging. "I guess that answers the question of why you married me."

"I planned to steal your riches and make off with your castle once I was forced to kill you before you killed me. It would have been a grand plan, if all your gold hadn't been fake and your castle wasn't infested with a fae." I swung my feet, bracing my hands on either side of me. "The real question is why did you marry me? Did Reinhault force you to do it? Pretty sure that kind of coercion makes our wedding more than a little illegal, if you want to declare it to be so."

Why did my aching throat constrict at that? As if I didn't want all this to fall apart like that. But why? It wasn't as if I had married him intending to be, well, married.

"He forced me, yes, but not the same way he forced me to do…other things." Duke Guy gestured toward my neck, his gaze only lifting that high before he turned away once again. "Once I married, I was bound by our bargain. But until then, I was free to resist him. Thus he created the drought to force me into marriage another way. I would hold out, for a while, but in the end, he had me trapped. I either married, knowing I was condemning the poor girl to death, or I refused and watched as hundreds of people all across the kingdom starved to death." Duke Guy hunched farther over the hands he braced against the battlements, his head hanging. "He placed the choice of who died in my hands, knowing I would bear the guilt either way."

I waited, sensing the duke had more to say. He had held all this inside for years, and now that it was spilling out, there was no stopping the flood.

"The drought got worse every time. The first drought only affected Gysborn, and that was bad enough. I held out for three years, hoping I could weaken him by denying him the blood he needed." Guy shook his head, his back shaking under his exhale. "In the end, I could stand the suffering of my people no longer, and he got his way. I married a local girl from the village. An orphan who had no one and had stars in her eyes at the prospect of marrying so high above her station. I told myself I could protect her."

"But you couldn't. He had you too tightly bound." It was

hard, keeping my voice to a gentle whisper. I wasn't used to being soft or gentle. But Guy was too fragile for a booming laugh or witty banter right now.

"I have some fae blood in me. Just a trace, but enough that he figured out how to bind me." The duke's fingers dug into his beard, as if searching out the scar that was hidden beneath. "Don't ask me how. My human blood should have protected me from such things, and yet he still bound me."

I waited, wondering if I should leave my perch to put an arm around him. That was the action of a wife, after all.

But I wasn't sure what I was to him. Nor what he was to me.

He curled even more in on himself, the battlements the only thing keeping him upright. "That second drought was worse. It spread to the surrounding dukedoms. The king raised the taxes to pay for the aid sent to the affected villagers, and when his assessor saw the lavish decorations and filled vaults, the levy he placed on Gysborn became far too high. Yet I couldn't give the king the fool's gold. Yes, it looks real enough to those without the gift to see past the glamor while it is in the confines of Gysborn. But it turns to pyrite the moment it is taken past our borders. And the bargain would not allow me to explain the truth to the king."

And that was where I came in, robbing the tax collections he'd scraped together and giving the money back to the villagers. "Surely there was a better way than heaping more misery on your people?"

"Was there?" Duke Guy's head shot up, and he shot me a glare, as if he just remembered that he was spilling his secrets to the Hood, not his wife. "What was I supposed to do? At first, I did fund the taxes with my own money. But that was soon exhausted, between paying the taxes and buying shipments of grain to feed the people. If I didn't pay, the king would have swooped in and tried to take the money by force.

He might have condemned me and the entire village as traitors for refusing to pay the taxes. He has certainly threatened mass hangings enough times when taking me to task about the Hood's actions and the people's loyalty to the outlaw."

I winced, staring at my hands. Duke Guy had been right all along. I really had made things worse by becoming the Hood.

The duke kept talking, as if he planned to ignore the fact that I was the Hood for a little while longer. "More than that, Reinhault would have simply weaseled his way into a bargain with the new duke. Or, perhaps, he would have set his sights higher and sought a bargain with the king himself. As long as he was content toying with me and as bound to me as I was to him through our bargain, then I had him as contained as possible."

Not a great choice. But, then again, he'd had precious few options, all of them bad.

"For three years I held out, watching the drought eat away at dukedom after dukedom. People were dying. Law and order started breaking down. In some of the neighboring villages, slavers started preying on the poorest of the people under the guise of indentured servitude. It was all I could do to keep such men out of Gysborn." His back hunched, as if saying the words added more weight to the burden he carried.

I had hated the heavy fist he'd used in ruling this dukedom. But it seems I hadn't understood its purpose. In the end, he'd rallied the people and kept the peace. Not by gaining their loyalty, but by earning their utter hatred so that they unified against him.

"This time, Reinhault saw my resolve to not endanger another girl. So when a nobleman and his daughter passed through Gysborn, Reinhault saw to it that I was scandalously alone with her for quite some time. Nothing happened, but it was enough to force a marriage anyway. The more I begged her father not to force the marriage, the more determined he became that everything must be set right with a marriage." Guy's voice dropped low. "She was dead within two months. By that point, her father had also passed away suddenly, so there was no one to protest her death to the king."

Likely another death we could blame on Reinhault.

I tapped my heels against the stone wall as I swung my legs. "And that's why you proposed marriage to me so quickly when I showed up on your doorstep, claiming to be a noblewoman traveling with my father in a near repeat of that history. If you didn't, Reinhault would've done his best to put us in a compromising position to force a marriage."

Never knowing that a marriage was exactly what I had been scheming for as well.

"Yes. And by this point, I knew his tendency toward escalation. I feared whatever situation he devised would involve more than merely locking us in a closet for most of the day." Duke Guy shivered yet again, as if imagining just what horrors the fae would have forced him to do to secure a marriage. "These past two years of drought were the worst of all. The entire kingdom has been suffering from it, and it is spreading beyond our borders. All those deaths. All those suffering people. And it is all my fault."

This was the topic he'd avoided, even as he'd talked about the deaths of his second and third wives.

And yet, this was the most important part of all. The bargain and how it had led to the death of his first wife.

"What was the bargain?" I spoke softly. The bargain couldn't be what Reinhault had made it out to be. Maybe Guy had been a different person back then, but I couldn't see him agreeing to a bargain as the fae had worded it back in that room.

Guy gave another one of those bitter laughs, his head

hanging until his forehead nearly touched his fisted hands. "You'd think, for something that unleashed so much horror, that I would remember every word with crystal clarity. But I don't. I was young. Foolish. I had just become the duke after my parents suffered what I had assumed was a tragic accident."

But it hadn't been. It had been the start of Reinhault slowly working his way into a position of power and control.

Guy sucked in a breath, and when he exhaled, his first wife's name came out laced with tears, even if I couldn't see them in the darkness. "Camille. We were so desperately in love, and life seemed so full, even with mourning for my parents. When this fae approached me one day and offered me the world, I took it."

I remained silent. He had made a foolish decision, but I was in no position to judge.

"All I could think about was giving Camille better than the shabby furnishings and decrepit castle I'd inherited from my parents. Gysborn has never been the wealthiest of dukedoms, and this was my chance to change that for the sake of my beloved wife and our future dreams together." Guy's voice grew even more choked. "When Reinhault tied the bargain to my wife being a perfect wife, I didn't think anything of it. She was flawed and human and all the things that made her perfect in my eyes. It wasn't until later that I realized it wasn't my definition of perfect that went into the bargain but Reinhault's twisted one."

This probably wasn't the moment to feel a stab of something almost like jealousy along with the compassion. But it seemed my heart wasn't listening.

"I fought so hard to save her. That was when Reinhault gave me this scar." Guy traced a line in his beard along the side of his jaw. "It was a taunt. That all I suffered was a cut on my face while my wife lay dead at my feet."

"I'm sorry." It was so pitiful, compared to everything he'd told me.

Guy flattened his palms against the stone, drawing in ragged breaths. "Camille. Lucy. Allison. None of them deserved to die. It should have been me. I was the one who made the bargain. I should have suffered the consequences. Instead, I was turned into their executioner. And Camille..." He was weeping now, even as he kept talking. "She loved me. Even as I put the noose over her head. Even as I..."

He broke then, collapsing against the wall and sliding down until he huddled on his knees.

I pushed off my perch and went to him. I'd never held a man while he cried, and I wasn't sure how to go about it. Sure, I'd seen my brothers cry plenty when they'd been boys. We'd all cried a good bit when we'd found our parents dead.

Guy was neither my brother nor a young boy. And I wasn't the kind of woman given to affectionate hugs and soothing words.

But he was a man long-tortured and burdened by a grief he had not been free to feel until now. I had to do something, even if it didn't feel as natural or as comfortable to me as swaggering through the forest with the bow in my hand.

Yet as I knelt in front of him, wrapped my arms around him, and cradled the back of his head with a hand buried in his hair, it didn't feel quite so unnatural after all.

I thought of those three dead women who had also been married to this man. Allison, a woman forced into marriage by the men in her life and killed by a cruel fae. Lucy, a girl from the village who had jumped at the chance for a better life, only to die far too young.

And Camille. A wife who had deeply loved her husband, as he had loved her.

He held onto me and wept. Those deep, wracking sobs

probably hurt the wound in his chest, especially as he'd ditched the sling in his turmoil of the past few minutes.

After long minutes, he drew himself together, pushing away from me to sit with his back to the stone battlements. He dragged his hands over his face, though if he looked all red-eyed and messy, I couldn't see in the shadowed darkness. He spoke between his fingers. "I suppose this is one more shame for you to add to my account."

I sat next to him, our shoulders not quite touching. "You and I have plenty to be ashamed of when it comes to the past few years. But those tears aren't one of those things. Don't you think that Camille, Lucy, and Allison deserve a few tears?"

"Yes, they do." Guy rested his head against the wall behind him, tilting his face toward the starlit sky far above us.

I gave him a few more moments to collect himself before I asked, "Well, now what do we do? About us, I mean. You and me. Our marriage."

"Each of us went into this believing we would have to kill the other. That is hardly the foundation for a marriage." He scrubbed a hand over his face again, his fingers tugging at his beard.

"No, I guess it isn't. But that piece of paper we signed is still rather legal and binding." I toyed with the hem of my dress. It was rather ragged, after everything I had put it through that day. How I wanted my trousers, shirt, and cloak. I wanted to pull my hood over my head and feel bold and strong once again. I cleared my throbbing throat, not looking at him. "I suppose you still need an heir."

He gave a snort, that hand over his face still obscuring his expression. "That is the least of my concerns right now. My bloodline can die out and the dukedom revert to the king for all I care."

Well that was one worry off the table. If we made something out of this marriage, it wouldn't be because of that cold pressure. If we got to that point, it would be because we loved each other and wanted that future.

I shifted, stretching my legs out in front of me. It wasn't that ladylike while wearing this dress, but it was too dark for anyone to care. I lowered my voice so that any patrolling guards wouldn't overhear, even if they had given us plenty of privacy so far. "What about the fact that I am the Hood? I know what your duty to the law demands when it comes to me. I tried my best not to, but I know I killed men during some of my robberies. I deserve to hang."

He stiffened, his hand dropping from his face, and he tipped his face toward me, his gaze so burning I could see the glint even in the darkness. "I know it denies justice, and perhaps it makes me a weak man unfit to hold my title. But I can't watch another wife hang."

I could hear the rasping pain in his voice. I had fought this man for years, and I knew his sense of justice. It killed him to let the Hood go with no consequences. Yet, it would kill him more to give the order for my hanging.

I touched my neck, wincing at the scrape of my fingers against the tender, bruised skin. "I guess I did hang. I didn't die of the hanging, but perhaps the thought of it will assuage some of your guilt in letting me go free."

In the torchlight, I could see the way his grimace twisted his face. "I'm not sure I can ever picture that as justice. Those moments as I placed the noose around your neck..." He shuddered, squeezing his eyes shut for a moment as he drew in deep breaths that seemed to steady him. "And to think I longed to see the Hood hang, never knowing what it would cost if I did."

I had, on my darker days, thought about what it would be like mounting the steps to the gallows, staring at a shouting crowd and seeing Guy's cold eyes as he gave the order for them to drop the trap door.

It wasn't a pleasant thought, and I never liked to dwell on unpleasant things for long. It had never happened, and never would now.

I traced my fingers over the bruises on my neck again. "What will you tell the king?"

The king was still hunting me. He wouldn't so easily let the Hood go, even if Guy was prepared to do so.

"I'll have to report all of this to the king, now that I am free to tell him Reinhault was fae. Enough of the king's soldiers stationed here saw Reinhault's ears. They will confirm my story." Guy gestured down to the courtyard below where the coals of Reinhault's pyre still glowed. "Let the guilt for the Hood's crimes rest on his head as well. He paid far too little for his crimes in life. He might as well bear the guilt in death."

"I guess that is for the best." I couldn't help the sour note in my tone. Sure, I was glad not to hang. And I probably shouldn't be proud of what I had done as the Hood.

But it seemed wrong to have the actions of the Hood, the people's hero, given over to that fae monster Reinhault.

Guy gave something like a low laugh. "Don't sound so melancholy about it. I'll only insinuate that to the king. The villagers here are free to keep believing that their hero melted back into the shadows from whence he came."

I relaxed, resting a hand on my quiver. "Good." I'd spent too long building the Hood into a hero to have him turned into a villain like Reinhault.

Guy glanced at me, his gaze searching my face in the low light. "The king will only believe my story if the Hood halts his crimes at the same time as Reinhault's death." He paused, then asked in a lower, quieter voice, "Will the Hood stop his criminal activities?"

I drew in a deep breath and stared at the stars for a long moment. I'd loved being the Hood. I loved the adventure. I loved thinking that I was helping people.

But I had never been as heroic as I had imagined. It was time for me to set aside the cloak and release the Hood to the place where myths and legends lived on in hearts and imaginations. Perhaps he would do far more good as a story than I had ever managed in real life. Maybe that was the true fitting end to the Hood.

"Yes." My voice was just as quiet and low as his had been a moment ago. "Yes, the Hood and his merry men are done."

Guy released a long exhale, his gaze swinging back to the stars overhead once again. "Then you and your brothers are free to go. I suppose, after justice has been so long denied for what I have done, I can spare such mercy to you and them."

I patted my quiver and swiveled to better face him. "Reinhault was a fae. That makes him the jurisdiction of the foresters. And I have dispensed a forester's justice on him... and on you." When Guy sat up a little straighter and turned back to me, I gestured first to the courtyard, then at him. "For his sadistic murders, Reinhault was given an iron broadhead to the heart. For your foolishness in making a fae bargain, you suffered a practice arrow to the shoulder. As you said before, let the guilt rest on Reinhault's head and leave it at that."

He gave a small nod and faced the stars once again.

For a long moment we simply sat there, comfortable in the quiet peace of the night.

I sighed and sprawled my legs out in front of me again. "You never answered my question. What happens now? With us? Our marriage?"

"You have two options, Robin." Guy's gaze flicked toward me, but he didn't turn his head fully. "Regardless of what you decide, I will protect you from your past as the Hood. You have my word on that."

He was making sure I knew that he wasn't going to coerce me in any way.

I waited for what he had to say. I knew what I wanted. Strangely, it wasn't the option I would have chosen a month ago.

"Your first option is that you can leave, and I won't stop you. As I said, I am fine without an heir. You are free to return to the Greenwood and build whatever life you wish." Guy was carefully not looking at me.

We would still be married, and neither of us would be able to move on until the other died.

But he was offering me my old life back. I could return to the Greenwood and be a forester.

And yet, it wasn't what I wanted. Not anymore. "And what is the second option?"

This time, Guy faced me, and he held his hand out in the space between us. "You stay here. With me."

The words hung between us on the night air with an alluring kind of danger.

I wasn't going to make it that easy on him by giving my answer right away.

"Will I have to wear dresses all the time?" I gestured at the ratty remains of the dress I was wearing. If talking with him hadn't been so important, I would have marched back to my room and changed into my shirt and trousers long before now.

His mouth twisted into an expression that was somewhere between a wry smile and a grimace. "No, not unless you wish to do so. Or we are visiting the king's court. I have seen you in velvet. You wear it like a queen. You don't have to feel daunted at the prospect of facing the king and the nobles."

I snorted. "Do you really think I'm scared of facing all those petty nobles and their fancy ways? Sure, they might scorn me for not being noble born, but just think of all those thinly veiled insults to return with banter of my own? It sounds utterly thrilling. Though, I suppose walking across the table is frowned upon when it's the king's table."

Guy's wry smile dropped into something more like a glower. "It's always frowned upon no matter whose table it is, but more so when that table belongs to the king."

"Thought so." I smoothed my skirt in an exaggeratedly proper manner. "Then I will content myself with the fun there is to be had trading barbs with the ladies and lords."

Guy groaned and leaned his head against the stone once again. "I think we will visit the king as infrequently as possible."

I grinned. If I was going to set aside the Hood, then life as a duchess sounded like it would provide a wealth of adventure instead.

Perhaps Duke Guy and I might destroy each other. We were both leaders. Both independent. Both stubborn, even if he was stubbornly law-abiding and I was stubbornly feral. We would either make a well-matched team or we would consume each other.

Ah, but it would be such a thrill to find out which it was.

"So you don't want to tie me down?" I smirked at him, tapping my quiver once again as if to remind him of just what a wild thing he was bringing into his life.

He met my gaze then with such a fervent light in his eyes that it stole my breath in a way I'd never experienced before. "Never, Robin. Never. I want you to *soar*. Within the bounds of law and order, of course."

He'd said my name. Not just *my lady*, as if I was this faceless, nameless person he was holding at a distance. But he'd looked me in the eyes and said my name as if he savored it. I kept my teasing grin in place. "Law, yes. Order, no."

He tipped his head back and barked a laugh. It was such a genuine, open sound that it was unexpected, coming from him. After a moment, his laughter faded, and he pressed a hand over his bandaged wound. He held out his other hand to me again. "Does this mean that you will stay?"

I slid my hand into his, and it felt strangely right to lace my long and calloused fingers with his even longer and stronger ones. "Yes, of course I'm staying. After all the trouble I went through to claim this castle as my own, I'm not about to give it up."

He raised his eyebrows at me. "Even if it's falling apart and comes with a duke who doesn't have a coin to his name?"

"Even then." I waved at the courtyard. By now, the embers of the pyre had burned down to just a hint of red against the black night. "This was the place of the Hood's greatest triumph. I am not about to let that go."

He gave a shake of his head, his beard glinting a liquid orange in the torchlight. "A part of me still can't believe you are the Hood. I knew you were no lady from the moment I met you. Your manner of speech was wrong, and no lady would be caught dead in such a dated dress. Not to mention your brother was a very unconvincing maid."

"I knew his lack of acting skills was going to give us away." I muttered, earning another smile from Guy.

"It wasn't only *his* acting skills." Guy gave me a pointed look. "I knew you were playing some con, but I never guessed that you were the Hood. I had it so fixed in my mind that the Hood was a man. I hated him, and yet, in a strange way, he gave me hope. Chasing the Hood kept me sane and gave me a chance to put Reinhault's focus onto someone else for a few hours. The Hood had the freedom to help the villagers and frustrate Reinhault, even if it wasn't the law-abiding way to go about it."

It seems Guy had needed the chase as much as I had. I'm not sure either of us would have known what to do, if we had ever actually caught each other back then.

With my hand still in Guy's, I tried to read the tension in his grip. "It must be a bit galling, to find out the outlaw who outmanned you is really a woman."

Even as I spoke, Guy shook his head emphatically. "No. If anything, it shows that I have the good sense to be married to the only person capable of besting me. You've been here all of two weeks, and you already managed to eliminate my greatest enemy. You truly are a legend."

I tossed my head back and gave in to the hearty laugh filling my chest. "Most of that legendary status was good story-telling by my brother Alan. The Hood was always part me and part imagination."

"You still split my arrow and won the archery contest. You shot Reinhault through the heart even while being hanged. Don't sell yourself short." Guy gave my hand a gentle squeeze as he held my gaze.

"Oh, I have too much self-confidence to ever do that." I enjoyed another, softer laugh. I called it self-confidence. Will, when he was particularly peeved at me, called it arrogance. Perhaps it was a bit of both. I sobered and searched Guy's face once again. "I can ask Alan to turn his story-telling skills toward crafting a new narrative for you. You can be the hero and not the villain as you have been portrayed."

"No." Guy's smile twitched his beard even while his eyes remained solemn. "The people love the Hood. Frustrating as I find it, they need the hope having a hero gives them. I can't take that away, even now. Even if you no longer reprise your role of the Hood, he needs to live on in hearts and imaginations. To do that, he needs a villain to fight. And I'm not about to give that role over to Reinhault any more than you are willing to let him be the Hood. I'd rather he remain my bumbling minion where, in story at least, I'm the one giving the orders."

My heart gave a painful squeeze. Guy would rather remain a villain in the stories if it meant reclaiming some agency over what had happened to him.

"Besides," Guy's tone lowered, "I rather like my starring role in your story, even if it is as the villain."

It was the sweetest thing he'd ever said to me, melting something inside me that had never softened before. Perhaps we would have a chance. Eventually.

He needed time to grieve. I needed time to figure out how to set aside the Hood.

Guy lifted our clasped hands, bending as if he was going to kiss the back of my knuckles. Yet, he halted short of planting that kiss, and instead he let our hands drop with a sigh. "I'm sorry. I can't...I don't know if..."

"I know." I gave him a light punch to the shoulder.

As he gave me a slightly confused look, I wasn't sure my gesture worked. Perhaps I had been living in the woods with my six brothers for too long. A punch on the arm always seemed to work for them.

Guy had been through horrible suffering in the past eight years. He had loved his past three wives, even if that love had been the love of duty and honor for two of them and true love for his first wife Camille. Of course, he needed time to grieve them before he could even think of a future with me.

Besides, I needed time just as much. I hadn't planned for this marriage to last more than a few weeks. It would take time for me to get my heart and my head into the right place.

Neither of us was sure if he would ever love me or if I would ever love him. We didn't know if we could build a true marriage. To be honest, neither of us even knew if we would manage to be good platonic partners.

But he needed me. He needed my help with the villagers. They hated him, but they loved me. He needed a wife who understood Reinhault's atrocities and their cost. And, more than anything, he needed someone to badger him into living again.

And I needed him. I needed his protection from my past as the Hood and his moral compass to steer me into a more honorable future. No matter what that future looked like, I would have Guy. Fighting him had been one of the best parts of being the Hood. He'd been my antagonist for so many years that I couldn't imagine my life without him in it.

Chapter Thirteen

Yes, yes. I can hear your questions. Did Guy and I ever fall in love? That is the point of tales like this. It just wouldn't be complete without that happily ever after, now would it?

In the end, my ultimate heist would be stealing the duke's heart. It wouldn't be easy. Hearts weren't like gold. I couldn't just waltz in, grab it out of a vault, and make my escape. Hearts could only be handed over willingly, and Guy had locked his up tight.

I didn't know how to flirt or bat my eyes or pretend maidenly weakness. Not to mention, I'd always heard you should never compete with a dead woman for a man's affection. And I was competing with three.

So I set out to do what I did best. Annoy him until he couldn't picture his life without me.

Sure, it probably wasn't the correct way to go about falling in love. But you know me. If there was a right way and a wrong way to go about doing things, I would pick the wrong way.

But I would do it with style.

Whistling, I picked the lock on the duke's door, juggling the two cloth-wrapped bundles of our breakfasts, and let myself inside. I sauntered across the sitting room and flung open the door to the duke's bedchamber. "Rise and shine!"

In the grey light of pre-dawn, he was a lump underneath the covers. As I strolled across his room, once again whistling, he groaned and pulled his pillow over his head.

I hopped onto the end of the bed, causing the feather mattress to puff and the bed to shake. I walked across the bed and plopped down next to the headboard.

Guy lay on his back, the covers pulled to his chest. The little bit of his shoulders and chest that showed above the blankets were bare, giving me a glimpse of the scar from where I'd shot him.

Ah, yes. I loved waking him up all tousled and sleep-addled. I grinned and wiggled deeper into the pillows I'd piled on what I'd claimed as my side of the bed, even if I didn't sleep there. Yet.

"Robin…" Guy gave another groan, lifting the pillow just enough to peek at the window before he pulled it tight over his head once again. "The sun hasn't even risen yet."

"Rise with the birds, that's what I always say." I opened one of the breakfast bundles. I passed over the egg and ham sandwiched between two pieces of bread in favor of the apple. I polished the apple on my shirt.

"Pest," Guy moaned into his pillow. "Menace."

"Ah, such lovely endearments to hear from my husband's lips." I bit into the apple, causing a loud crunch. "It just melts my heart."

He cringed as I took another, even louder bite of the apple. His voice was muffled as he mumbled, "If you're going to keep doing this, you might as well just sleep in here."

I tensed, then forced myself to relax. This was what I had been angling toward these past mornings of annoying him awake. I wasn't going to hesitate if he invited me to take the leap.

Besides, I'd already picked out the prime spot on the fireplace mantle where I would put the pyrite arrow. Right where it would taunt him by being one of the first things he saw in the morning.

As if realizing what he'd just said, Guy froze and slowly peeled the pillow from over his face to peer up at me.

I grinned and spoke around a mouthful of apple. "Fine by me. It would be so much easier to ruffle your feathers if I didn't have to trek across half the castle to do it. Just think how much earlier I could wake you up."

With another groan, Guy pressed the pillow back to his face. "Forget I said anything."

"Too late. You can't take it back." I rotated the apple in my hand, focusing on it rather than on him.

Guy's voice dissolved into indecipherable muttering.

Mission accomplished.

I smacked the pillow where it rested above his face. "It's time to get up. We're going to have another monster attack today. I can feel it."

He set aside the pillow and heaved a sigh, blinking blearily up at me. Shortly after Reinhault's death, Guy had shaved off his beard. Neither of us had liked his look clean-shaven, so he'd grown back a goatee, leaving most of the scar along his jaw visible. Proof of what he'd survived at Reinhault's hands.

I was kind of envious that I hadn't gotten any cool scars. You'd think nearly getting your neck stretched would have left some visible scar, but nope. Such a letdown.

Guy pushed back the covers and rolled to his feet. He

wore a pair of rumpled trousers, but his torso and feet were bare.

I took in the sight of his muscled back. Now this was the view that I came here every morning to see. It would be a lot more convenient once I moved in here. Still staring, I took a slow, deliberate bite of my apple.

"Nuisance." With one last glare in my direction, Guy opened his wardrobe, the large oak door hiding all but his feet from sight. After a moment of searching, he poked his head around the door. "Robin, where is my black shirt?"

I smirked at him and took a final bite of the apple. He knew very well that I wasn't going to tell him where I'd hidden it. "Wear the red one. It still has a bloodstain the laundress couldn't get out after the last monster attack, and it will just get mucked up again today."

"Outlaw." He disappeared behind the large wardrobe door once again.

It probably wasn't that mature of me, but I hadn't entirely been able to stop the stealing. One step at a time and all that. Instead, I only stole from him. It was just the odd shirt or favorite dagger, and I always returned them. Eventually. But it was just too fun to rile him a bit.

"You could always put a new lock on your door." I set aside the apple core and picked up the egg, ham, and bread sandwich.

"I could. But a new lock would be a hassle for me to open every day." I could hear him rummaging in his wardrobe again, even if I couldn't see him.

"Or you could put bars on your window." I chomped a large bite of breakfast. On some mornings, I climbed the castle and entered his room through the window. Just to keep things interesting.

"And interrupt that view? I don't think so."

"A new lock on that wardrobe might stop me from touching your things."

"It would be a bother to unlock every time I needed a change of clothing." Guy peeked around the edge of the wardrobe door, meeting my gaze for a moment, before he ducked out of sight again.

I settled deeper into the pillows, satisfied now that I had assured him that he could ask me to stop, if he wished, and he had confirmed he wasn't truly annoyed.

See? We were doing so well on this healthy relationship and all that. Proper communication was key.

He changed into his clothes for the day, using the open door of the wardrobe as a changing screen, and I only caught the occasional glimpse of his arm or his head. I wasn't sure whose blushing sensibilities he thought he was protecting, but it certainly wasn't mine.

When he was finished, he shut the wardrobe door. He was dressed in black trousers and a red shirt that would look exceptionally war-like when he put on his weapons.

I quickly swallowed a final bite of my breakfast, ignoring the way it went down hard through my tight throat. After stuffing the unfinished half of my breakfast back into the wrappings for later, I grinned and held up the second breakfast bundle. "Hungry?"

He took a wary step toward the bed.

As soon as he moved, I rolled to my feet, gripping his breakfast in one hand.

He huffed a sigh. "Do we have to do this every morning?"

"Not every morning." I eyed him, gauging what way he would move. "Just often enough to keep the morning thrilling."

When he lunged for me, I dodged around him, darting to the far side of the bedchamber. He raced after me, giving a low frustrated growl as I evaded a snatching hand.

I laughed, my heart beating faster in my chest, my head whirling with the rush of the chase.

It seemed I would always need to be chased by this man, even if the end consequences would be less deadly than they would have been before.

He finally snagged an arm around my waist. As I laughed even harder, he reeled me in, swinging me off my feet to place my back to the wall. He braced his arms on either side of me, trapping me yet not menacing.

For a moment, we faced each other only inches apart, both of us panting and grinning.

"It seems you have bested me, Duke." I pressed against the wall behind me.

He stepped in closer, though he didn't touch me. "Do I get to claim my reward, Robin Hood?"

I held up his cloth-wrapped breakfast in the space between us. "Yes. Your breakfast."

His fingers closed over mine on the bundle, and he drew the barrier of our joined hands out of the way. "I was thinking of something…more."

"Oh really?" Now I was sagging against the wall, my voice coming out more breathy than boisterous.

Only an inch remained between our faces, our breaths mingling. With one hand still wrapped around mine, Guy leaned his other hand on the wall next to my head. His voice was a low, shivering whisper. "I would really love to kiss you."

That was all the invitation I needed. I wasn't the type to wait for him to do the kissing first. I fisted my hand in his shirt, pulled him the last inch, and kissed him as an outlaw would. Passionately. Roguishly. Just a little bit arrogantly.

When I pulled back, I whispered near his ear, "I know you love me."

He gave a throaty laugh, brushing a kiss to my temple. "You don't even know how much you'll love me."

With that, he drew me in for a deeper, longer kiss. It made me believe that, perhaps, this law-abiding duke had just a little of the outlaw in him. After all, his theft of my heart had been a heist worthy of the Hood herself.

Fighting Monsters and Falling in Love, Robin Hood Style

BONUS SHORT STORY

A loud knock on the duke's door broke through the haze of kissing.

I pushed back from Guy and shoved the bundle of his breakfast at his chest, and he fumbled to take it from me by reflex. Smirking, I ducked under his arm. "What do you want to bet that is the messenger telling us there's a monster attack?"

"I know better than to bet against you."

"Smart man." I strolled from Guy's bedchamber, crossed the sitting room, and yanked open the door.

The messenger stood there, hand raised for another knock. He blinked at me and cleared his throat. "I...hope I'm not interrupting anything."

My smirk widened. "Not at all. Actually, the duke will be quite grateful that you saved him from my annoying presence."

The servants knew I invaded Guy's bedroom each morning. After all, the cook packed two breakfasts for me each morning with a twinkle in her eyes. I was just thankful to see the joy return to the servants. They, too, had suffered under Reinhault.

As Guy's footsteps crossed the room behind me, I brushed past the messenger. "I'll have them ready the horses while you eat breakfast."

Guy muttered something under his breath behind me, but I didn't bother to listen.

The leather of my dress flapped against my legs as I strode down the stairs. The skirt was divided into four panels with slits up to my thighs that revealed the trousers I wore underneath. It was a nod to feminine attire while also letting me comfortably ride astride. Not to mention that the leather helped protect against scratches and venom while fighting monsters.

In the courtyard, I found the stablehands had already gone ahead and saddled Guy's bay and my black. A maid even showed up to hand me my sword, quiver, and unstrung bow, all while grinning as if she'd been given a great honor to fetch my weapons for me. Perhaps the castle folk were getting used to their duke and duchess hurrying off to fight monsters at every opportunity.

Munch waited in the courtyard next to the small brown horse he'd been provided from the castle stables. Now that the foresters were official again—their disbandment was another thing to blame on Reinhault—John, Will, and Munch had all been issued horses to aid them in fighting monsters and in contacting the duke quickly in case of a major monster attack.

Which all of them tended to be lately, as Reinhault had predicted.

"How much fun is waiting for us in the Greenwood?" I sidled up to Munch and held out the other half of my breakfast sandwich.

He took it, glared at the spots where I'd bitten into the

sandwich, before he started eating from the other side. "It is going to be a wild one. Monsters are coming through circles left, right, and center."

"Perfect." I took the reins of my black gelding from the stablehand. "I love a good monster battle in the morning. It starts the day out right."

Munch stuffed the rest of the sandwich into his mouth, talking as he chewed. "You'd better pack a lunch. I think this is going to be more like an all-day affair."

"Even better." I knew I was grinning from ear-to-ear, but I couldn't help it.

Guy strode from the castle, wearing his own sword, quiver, and bow, along with a few assorted knives. There was just something about him all dolled up in weapons that made me want to go over there and kiss him.

Monster battle first. Kissing later.

I took the time to string my bow, and Guy did the same, as our guards assembled around us. We had a much smaller force now that the king's soldiers had been recalled. Not to mention a few of the more mercenary and cruel soldiers that had been recruited by Reinhault had been released to go their separate ways. The guards we had left were a good bunch. After all, they took orders from me without question, even during the heat of battle.

We rode from the courtyard at a canter with Guy and me leading the way.

THE COOL, green embrace of the Greenwood wrapped around us as we entered the main road cutting through the forest. A squad of our soldiers had been detached to guard the village, in case any of the fae monsters made it through the forest and thought to make a snack out of some hard-working farmer lad.

Munch gestured ahead of us. "Will is defending the largest circle, but John did a sweep and spotted monsters coming from some of the other circles."

"In that case, Munch, you'd better lead a squad of men toward the maple and mushroom circle. Point another squad of soldiers in the direction of the rock circle while you're at it." I scanned the forest around us, searching for any signs of monsters. My senses were tingling, the forest carrying an underlying sickly, sweetness of fae magic that told me their realm and our world were particularly close today. "Guy, you and I will reinforce Will."

Guy gave a sharp nod, then barked out his orders to his men, dividing up the squads. They saluted and turned their horses toward their assigned destinations.

My black horse eagerly bounced into a fast trot as Guy and I led the way deeper into the Greenwood until we neared the spot where I had pulled off my last heist of a tax shipment all those months ago shortly before I married Guy.

Instead of a tax wagon sitting in the middle of the rutted dirt track, a five-headed hydra blocked our path. Its tan, scaled body was as thick as some of the medium-sized oaks surrounding us while darker brown diamond markings ran along its back from its heads down to the huge rattle at the end of its tail. Each head was blunted with slitted eyes and fangs that carried venom.

As we approached, it hissed and raised its heads, its rattle sending up a deafening, high-pitched warning.

"Ah, now this is the perfect way to start the morning." I grinned as I halted my horse. Even with the hissing, many-headed snake monster in front of us, the black remained steady, only his pricked ears and low snorts giving away his nervousness.

"I thought tormenting me was your perfect morning." Beside me, Guy gripped his bow and selected an arrow from his quiver.

"This is just the icing on the rather sweet cake that this morning has turned out to be." I traced my fingers over my arrows until one of the black-fletched ones called to me.

The hydra slithered forward a few feet. We would have to take our shots now before it got too close.

There are only two ways to kill a hydra. Either you have to chop off all of its heads at the same exact time or you have to take it through the heart, a heart that is protected by a very thick layer of scales.

Guy stood in the stirrups, sighted past all the heads to the spot where the heads all came together. With intense focus, he released, sending the arrow zipping past the swirling heads to bury itself in the hydra's chest.

The hydra's heads reared back, more angry than hurt at the shot.

I only had a second. If I didn't get this shot right, then the now very angry hydra would attack. Standing in my stirrups, I sank into my instincts until the forest, the soldiers at my back, and even Guy at my side faded. It was only me and the hydra and the fletching of the arrow Guy had put into its chest above its heart.

I waited for a heartbeat until everything felt right. Then, I released.

My arrow sang in the morning air, the broadhead glinting in the light slanting through the leaves.

Then, it thunked into the hydra's chest, slicing into the same hole and sliding along Guy's arrow where my arrow would find least resistance. Since it didn't have to punch through the tough scales and layers of muscle that Guy's arrow had, the force carried my arrow far deeper until the broadhead pierced the monster's heart.

The hydra twisted and coiled, flailing in a squirming, shuddering death roll.

As soon as it went limp, two of the soldiers leapt from their horses, raced forward, and chopped at the body with large axes until all of the heads were separated from the thick body.

I dropped to the ground as well. "It will be too thick for the horses up ahead."

Guy nodded, and we left the horses with one of the soldiers.

We had to dispatch several smaller monsters as we tramped through the forest. The sounds of crashing and roaring and shouting came from ahead of us.

Breaking into a sprint, I raced through the forest, dodging trees and stepping around roots. This was my home. My feet knew these paths. I quickly outpaced Guy, and, for a moment, it was almost like old times. Me, leading the way on some merry chase. Him, crashing along in my wake and cursing my nimble feet.

The spruces that marked the fairy circle darkened the forest ahead of me. I broke through a thicker stand of underbrush and skidded to a halt in a relatively clear patch of knee-high hummocks of grass.

Shouting an inarticulate cry, Will brought his sword down, chopping off the head of a massive rat the size of a coyote. Behind him, my sister-in-law Angie stabbed her pitchfork at giant goat with rolling eyes and frothing mouth.

"Nice of you to join us." Will swiped his forehead on his sleeve, leaving a wet smear that contained just as much monster guts as sweat.

"You know I wouldn't miss all the fun!" I grinned as I selected an arrow, aimed, and shot the slavering goat monster through the eye, sending my arrow past its thick skull and into its brain.

"Fun is not what I would call it." Angie rolled her eyes and took a moment to lean on her pitchfork, panting from her exertion.

Contrary to her words, she had a smile on her face. Will had surprised all of us by up and marrying her only a few months after we had given up our outlaw ways. It turned out he'd been secretly carrying on a romance under our noses—and done such a good job of hiding it that even I didn't suspect.

I was happy for him. Angie had grown up in the village and had only needed a little bit of training to get her up to snuff on monster killing. She was still a little leery of having the infamous Duke Guy "Bluebeard" as her brother-in-law, but she was slowly warming to him.

With a crash, a gigantic monster burst from the faerie circle. The chimera had the head of a lion on one side, a goat's body complete with sharp, slashing hooves, and a tail tipped with a biting, hissing snake's head.

No more time for talking. I laughed and leapt into the fray, alternating between stabbing monsters with my sword, then shooting others with arrows. With Guy protecting my back—and me protecting his—we dispatched the monsters as they poured through the circle.

After an hour of fighting, I took aim at a harpy and let my arrow fly. The broadhead sank into the creature's chest, and it gave a sharp shriek before it plummeted from the sky.

My fingers danced over my remaining arrows. Only three left.

"Drop!" Guy shouted from somewhere to my right.

I didn't look at him. I simply dropped to the ground, holding my bow out to the side. Only heartbeats later, his arrows hissed through where I had been standing a moment earlier.

A yip came from the undergrowth to my left. Then a

snarling silver wolf burst from the forest, its fangs glinting in the afternoon sunlight, saliva dripping onto the forest floor. Guy's arrow stuck out of its shoulder, blood flowing stark and red against the fur of its right leg.

I only had time to roll onto my back before the wolf was upon me. As it slashed for my neck with its teeth, I grabbed its ruff with my left hand, holding those flashing teeth away from my face.

The wolf twisted its head and clamped its teeth around my forearm, its teeth sinking straight through my leather vambrace into my arm. Its legs scratched and tore at my legs and body, but the leather of my dress protected me from the worst of it.

Sucking in a sharp breath at the pain, I yanked out my knife. Pinned as I was, I couldn't get a lot of force behind my arm as I drove the knife into the wolf's belly.

At the same time, a thud and a blow knocked into the wolf, sending it sprawling with a yelp, my knife still sticking out of its body. I still gripped its ruff, unwilling to let it go even as it gave a few last shuddering breaths, then lay still.

"Robin!" Guy dropped to his knees next to me, reaching for me. His dark eyes swept over me, taking in the scratches before settling on my arm, where the bite mark oozed blood. "You're hurt."

I grimaced, let go of the dead wolf's fur, and pushed to a sitting position. "Just a little beat up and bloody is all. Though, I wouldn't mind washing out that bite on my arm as soon as possible. Never know where that wolf's mouth has been."

He rested his palm on my cheek, then eased his hand up to cradle the back of my head. "I shot too fast. I should have waited until I had a better shot, or taken my time with the shot. If I'd taken it in the chest instead of the shoulder—"

I placed my finger over his mouth, silencing him. I didn't

need him to get all guilty over a shot being less than perfect. "A bad shot once and a while happens to every archer, even us. You still got it, there at the end. With a little assist from me, of course."

"Of course." That put the smile back on Guy's face, though the deep worry lines still remained etched across his forehead.

"I'll be fine." I leaned forward and kissed his cheek in a spot that looked free of monster blood and guts. The prickle of dark stubble brushed against my lips. Not giving myself time to linger, I placed a hand on his shoulder and used him to leverage myself to my feet.

Once standing, I yanked my knife free of the wolf and glanced around as Guy stood next to me.

For the first time in hours, the forest around us was quiet, free of fae monsters.

"Do you think that was the last of them?" Guy retrieved my bow for me from where it had fallen a few feet away, handing it to me.

I closed my eyes and worked to access those honed senses. The swell of magic I'd been sensing all day had tapered off, leaving behind only the tang of blood and freshly dead carcasses. "I think so."

"Good." Guy took my arm and started unlacing the vambrace with deft fingers.

Now that the fight was over, weariness settled heavier over me. Enough that I let him work without an attempt at protesting banter.

He removed the vambrace, then peeled back the sleeve of my shirt, showing the puncture wounds from the wolf's teeth. They weren't deep, but they definitely would need cleaning.

"The medical gear is back with the horses." Guy placed a hand on my lower back, gently steering me in that direction.

It warmed something inside me, how focused he was on seeing to my injuries. But I dug in my heels. "Let's check on Will and Angie first. One of them might have been injured as well."

During the fighting, Guy and I had worked our way into the brush, just out of sight of the faerie circle.

When I took a step in that direction, Guy didn't protest. Though he did heave a deep sigh as he fell into step with me.

I pushed through the saplings and soon popped out into the cleared space. There, I found Will and Angie in each other's arms, kissing rather passionately.

Whoops. Never mind. They were obviously fine. I spun on my heels, running into Guy.

Before we could take another retreating step, another swell of magic came from the faerie circle with such strength that Will started and yanked away from Angie so fast that she gasped and stumbled.

I fumbled for one of my remaining arrows, nocking it just as five more of those gigantic rats leapt from the entrance to the faerie circle.

Next to me, Guy drew an arrow, aimed, and released in one smooth motion. One of the unusually large rodents squeaked and went down. My arrow took down a second rat only a heartbeat later.

As I reached for another arrow, I noted that two more two figures stepped from the arched entrance between the spruce trees. These were not monsters, but a fae man and woman.

Will's arrow slammed into a third rodent as the fae woman stepped forward and swung a shepherd's staff. She hooked the crook of it around a rat, pinning it in place.

She glanced up at us, her cheeks rosy with exertion and strands of her blond hair sticking to the perspiration on her face and neck. "Someone shoot this thing!"

I started. As the breeze swept her hair aside, I could see that her ears were rounded, not tapered.

She was a human, not fae. But what was she doing with the fae man? His ears were clearly tapered, sticking out through the tousled strands of his dark brown-black hair in a way that would have been adorable if he hadn't been one of those too handsome, far too dangerous fae.

The dark haired fae man stepped forward and swung a club at the fifth giant rat before the creature could bite his leg. He kept his other hand pressed over a bundle strapped to his chest.

Guy already had another arrow nocked, and he flicked his gaze to me. "I'll take the one she's pinning if you can shoot the other."

I nodded and nocked my second-to-last arrow, pretending my heart wasn't beating harder. Guy had given me the harder of the two shots. His target was pinned in place, even if it was too close to the human woman for comfort.

But the other rodent was still dodging and snarling around the fae man's legs. If I missed, I would hit him.

He was fae. Hitting him normally wouldn't be something that I would concern myself with.

But that bundle he was cradling protectively against his chest was a baby. And I wasn't about to shoot at someone carrying a baby, even if he was a fae.

Guy's arrow hissed, then thunked into the rodent, taking it through the neck and pinning the dying monster to the forest floor.

I raised my bow and drew the arrow, focusing on my moving target and trying to ignore the wounds weakening my arm. The fae man swung his club again, batting the creature aside. As it rolled on the forest floor, I released.

Just as the creature came to rest and paused for just a

BLUEBEARD AND THE OUTLAW

moment to gather itself, my arrow thunked into it, killing it where it lay.

The fae man released a loud breath, swiped his sleeve across his forehead, and stepped closer to the human woman. "Next time, we're taking Buddy's advice and leaving Addy behind with a babysitter."

"Not with Buddy, though. Not until she's older. He doesn't even have hands." The woman patted the baby's back and pressed a kiss to one chubby cheek. The baby still slept, despite all the commotion. "I have plenty of siblings. I'm sure one of them could babysit. Perhaps it would be best to wait until Addy is older to introduce her to the human realm."

Uh...I studied the little family in front of us and fingered my last arrow.

Glancing over, I met Guy's gaze. What were we supposed to do now? Fae were tricky. I couldn't trust these two. But it also didn't sit right inside me to aim an arrow at a man carrying a baby, even if he was fae.

Will also toyed with an arrow, but he didn't draw it from his quiver. Beside him, Angie held her pitchfork, though the tines were pointed at the forest floor.

Guy stepped forward and cleared his throat. "I'm Lord Guy of Gysborn, and this is my wife Lady Robin. We don't take kindly to fae in these parts. If you leave peaceably now, there won't be any trouble."

The human woman stepped to place herself between us and her child. The fae man gripped his club tighter. While he was dressed in a grey shirt and dark pants, she wore a light green dress with many layers to a skirt that ended, oddly enough, at her knees. Both of them wore some kind of formal looking coat, though his was black while hers was green.

The woman held out her hands to us, palm out. This time when she spoke, I could make out an accent that was local to the villages around the Greenwood. "Don't shoot. Please. We're not here to snatch anyone or do anything sneaky. We just want to talk." She reached up and drew her hair away from her ear, giving us an even better view of its rounded shape. "See. I'm human, just like you."

I studied her. I couldn't sense any fae illusion wrapped around her, but there had been so much fae magic swirling around this forest recently that something as subtle as a change to her ear could have been lost in the clamor. "State your business. And no funny stuff."

The woman drew her shoulders straighter. "I'm Meg. This is the Greenwood, isn't it? I come from a village on the far side of the forest from here, if Basil's calculations of where we'd end up are correct."

By the way she pointed at the fae man, I could gather that he was the Basil she mentioned.

"Yes, this is the Greenwood." With Guy still wary and guarding my back, I relaxed my stance and dropped my hand from my quiver. "What are you doing with the fae?"

"It's a long story. The short version is that I fled to the Fae Realm to escape a slaver and the drought, and Basil here is the one who helped me escape. Is the drought still plaguing the kingdom? Or has that been over and done for years and years? I have no idea how much time might have passed here." Meg glanced around the forest, its foliage lush and green. "Though, it doesn't look like the forest is suffering, so the drought must be over."

"Yes, the drought ended nine months ago." Was it dangerous that I was giving this information to the fae? Meg might be human, but Basil was definitely fae. "You said you wanted to talk?"

Basil stepped around Meg, one hand still resting on the baby's back. His accent was foreign and far more polished than hers. "We are librarians at the Great Library in the

Court of Knowledge. In the Fae Realm, we have been experiencing an unusually high number of monster attacks recently, and it has come to our attention that these monsters have been getting through into the human realm."

Meg huffed. "Incompetant Oberon can't even guard his own court, much less keep the monsters from wandering into the circles that connect to his side of the Tanglewood. I didn't realize how much we had to be thankful for, living on the side of the Greenwood that connects to the Court of Knowledge. I only had to worry about lonely fae librarians coming to snatch human brides, not fae monsters."

Meg and Basil shared a look, almost as if there was some inside joke between them.

Basil's smile turned even more lopsided. "Do you really want King Oberon to turn his attention onto the human realm?"

"No, probably not. Puck caused enough havoc last time before he finally returned to the Fae Realm." Meg heaved another loud sigh. "Still, why the Court of Revels puts up with such a buffoon is beyond me."

"He's better than the other options." Basil shrugged, then reached into an inside pocket of his coat. I tensed, but he only pulled out a roll of papers that seemed much too large to have fit in that pocket. "A few years ago, three of the especially cruel fae in our realm tried to stage a coup in the Court of Revels. Oberon and Titania fought them off—mostly because some of the other Courts stepped in to help—and these fae were banished to the human realm. Oberon, of course, failed to keep track of them after that."

I wasn't sure who this King Oberon was, but he did sound just as incompetent as Meg had said.

"Now that the Court of Knowledge is in a more secure position, my king has decided to track down those three fae. It was suspected that one or more of them might have gone through this circle." Basil gestured from Meg to himself. "Our king sent us since Meg was originally from this area and I have the protections that being bonded and married to her give me."

Ah, that was right. He and Meg were bonded in a way that could only happen if she had gone with him to the Fae Realm willingly. Basil enjoyed the protections that Reinahult had killed over and over again to obtain by his dark bargain and twisted ritual with the key and the hanging and the blood.

It made me more inclined to trust Basil and Meg. Surely such a bond could only form with a fae who was decent, as far as fae went.

I shared a glance with Guy. Could Reinhault have been one of those fae? He certainly had been cruel. Banishment from the Fae Realm would explain why he had come to Gysborn in the first place, why he had never chased me into the faerie circles while he had been the sheriff, and why he would have done his best to prevent anything else from the Fae Realm from coming through the circles and noticing where he'd set up his new lair.

I turned back to Basil and Meg. "We have experienced some fae related trouble here in Gysborn lately. What do these three fae look like?"

Basil held up the roll of paper. "I have paintings of each of them, if you would care to take a look?"

We would have to step closer to the fae and his human wife to do so. But I wasn't getting any uneasy feeling deep in the pit of my stomach. If anything, my senses were easing the longer I talked with them.

It only took a glance at Will to communicate that I wanted him to stay where he was in case this was a trap. Will nodded in response, his stance shifting ever so slightly in readiness to nock his arrow again if needed.

With Will guarding my back and Guy at my side, I strode across the intervening space.

As I drew closer, I touched the iron bar in my quiver and searched my senses for any clang of warning, any twinge that something wasn't right. All I got was a confirmation that what I saw before me was genuine.

Up close, I could see the way Meg's features—from her golden hair and firm chin to her wiry build—matched those of our kingdom, lending credence to her story that she had come from a village on the far side of the Greenwood.

Basil's dark brown eyes held a soft warmth that was far different than Reinhault's oily charm.

Besides, Basil held a sleeping baby in a cloth carrier against his chest. The baby had left a large spot of drool on the fabric of his grey shirt while the child's cherub cheeks and long, dark lashes melted something inside me. Tiny, tapered ears peeked through the tousled hair that wasn't quite as dark as Basil's nor as light as Meg's.

Maybe it was a weakness, but I just couldn't keep up my guard.

As Guy and I halted, Basil unrolled the papers, presenting us with a painting of a brown-haired fae with flinty edgy to his green eyes.

Guy shook his head. "Not him."

Meg grimaced. "Bother. We were hoping it would be him. He was the leader and the worst of the lot."

I raised my eyebrows. Could there possibly be a fae worse than Reinhault? I had a hard time picturing it.

Basil shuffled the papers, then unrolled the second painting for us.

My breath caught in my throat. The painting captured every glint of Reinhault's gold hair, that tilt to his sensuous mouth, the almost good-natured twinkle to his blue eyes.

Beside me, Guy paled, his throat working.

Even I had to swallow before I could choke out, "That's him. That's Reinhault."

Basil's dark brown eyes studied us. "I can see he did something terrible here. Where is he? King Theseus and Queen Hippolyta are prepared to send some of her swordmaidens to apprehend him if necessary."

"No need. He's dead." My voice strengthened, and I gripped my iron rod tighter. "I put the arrow into him myself."

"Then we cut off his head and burned the body." Guy's jaw tightened. "We had to be absolutely sure he was dead."

"I sec." If anything, Basil's gaze softened further, as if he understood from our words just how horrific Reinhault's deeds had been. "If you could, I would appreciate a report of what happened. King Theseus will want the full story, and I would like to add the record to the Great Library."

Since Guy didn't seem in any shape to agree, I nodded. "I'll put something together. But," I glanced to Meg, "you probably should know. Reinhault caused the drought."

Meg's eyes widened, and she glanced up at Basil. "Great. That's just great. I had fae trouble all along, and I didn't even know it."

Basil wrapped an arm around her waist, pulling her closer and kissing her temple. "I'm sorry."

"Not your fault. I blame Oberon. If he hadn't shoved his problems on someone else by banishing these fae to the human realm, none of this would have happened." Meg leaned into Basil.

"In theory, these fae should have been banished to the Realm of Monsters, not the human realm. They just wiggled through the cracks."

"Because Oberon is beyond incompetent." At Basil's look, Meg gave a roll of her eyes. "It's true. And I'm safe to say it out loud here in the human realm."

"You still shouldn't say it. For all we know, Puck could be lurking around here somewhere." Basil glanced around at the trees. I wasn't sure what he was looking for, but I also cast a wary glance at the forest around us.

"Reinhault arrived in Gysborn about ten years ago, and he started the drought nearly eight years ago now." Guy's voice was flat, not betraying any of the emotion lurking in those words. "He's been dead for nine months."

I eased closer to him and took his hand, giving his fingers a squeeze. Guy had come a long way in nine months, but the pain was still there.

"I'm glad he's dead and the drought is over. While we've made our home in the Fae Realm, it's a relief to know that the kingdom we left behind is no longer suffering." Meg's gaze dropped down to my arm, and her eyes widened. "Crusty cats, you're wounded! What are you doing standing around talking? Here, I have some salve and stuff in my pockets. I learned a while back to always travel with medical supplies."

Now that she mentioned it, my arm was throbbing worse than ever. I'd been too focused on fending off fae to register the pain for a while there.

Meg fished in an inside pocket of her coat, taking out a jar filled with some green goo, a stack of bandages, a bowl, and even a pot of steaming water, though I had no idea how that had gotten in a pocket. She handed each item over to Basil until he was juggling all the items for her.

Guy placed an arm around my waist, steadying me. Now that I thought about it, I was a little dizzy. I leaned into his solid warmth, my bow pinched between us.

I probably shouldn't accept something fae-made, but I was beginning to like Meg. Perhaps it was foolish, but I didn't resist as Meg took my arm and started using one of the bandages and the hot water to clean the wolf bite.

"Blundering bats, this is a nasty one. Good thing I have this fae gunk. The magic will heal this up right proper for you." Meg finished washing the wounds. Wordlessly, Basil opened the jar and held it out to her. She swiped her fingers through the goo, then smeared it over my arm.

I sighed as a cooling sensation washed over the heated, aching bites. Guy's arm tightened around my waist. When I glanced up at him, the muscle at the corner of his jaw was knotted, his eyes pained.

"I'm going to be fine. Legends don't get killed off by a measly fae wolf bite." I leaned my head against his shoulder. It was rather nice when he got all worried and let his guard down.

"That could get infected. And you don't know what kind of magic it might have gotten into you." Guy grimaced, his gaze swinging from me to Meg and Basil and back.

"Oh, don't fuss about that. This stuff will take care of all that." Meg swiped one last glob over the slashes. When Basil held out the bandages, she started wrapping them around my arm.

Basil met Guy's gaze. "Meg's right. We got that jar from the Order of Healers. They know what they're doing. They've healed me from a basilisk bite a while back. A mere wolf is nothing."

The set of Guy's shoulders relaxed a little, but not all the way. I doubted Guy would find that much reassurance in the word of a fae, no matter how harmless this Basil appeared to be.

When Meg tied off the bandage, I moved my arm and hand experimentally. "This feels great. Thank you." I drew in a deep breath, hardly believing I was about to make this offer. "Would the two of you like to come to our castle for dinner tonight? We can tell you the full story of what Reinhault did while we eat."

Meg glanced up at Basil. "We have the time, right? I'd love to eat good, ol' human food again."

Basil eyed us but nodded. "We should be all right getting back, I think."

"Then, yes, we accept." Meg's grin was warm. The kind of grin that invited me to grin back.

WE WERE A RATHER rowdy bunch gathered around the large, beat up table in the castle's dining room. While this table didn't have the polish of the glamor Reinhault had cast over it, it was still plenty sturdy and large enough to hold all of us gathered around it.

And we were a large group, by the time we had all of my brothers, my sister-in-law, the girl John was courting and was likely going to make my sister-in-law before the year was out, our guests, Guy, and me around it. We even had room for when more of my brothers started adding sisters-in-law to the family, not to mention nieces and nephews down the line.

Meg turned out to be just as fun as I'd figured. And Basil was surprisingly nice, for a fae.

Their daughter Addison was about the most adorable thing I'd ever seen. And I wasn't normally the type to go all melty over things like babies.

By the time dinner was over, Basil, Meg, Guy, and I had set up a system to keep in touch with each other. That way, we could share information back and forth about what was happening in our realms. After all, there were still two evil fae out there—fae that were just as bad as, or even worse than, Reinhault.

That evening, Guy and I walked Basil and Meg back to the faerie circle. The Greenwood was now bathed in moonlight, everything silver and a dusky dark green. Meg waved one last time before she, Basil, and Addy stepped into the circle and disappeared.

I released a long sigh and turned to Guy. "Their baby is so cute. I want one."

Guy made a choking noise, whipping toward me. "Pardon. What?"

"I want one." I lightly punched his shoulder as I sauntered past him, heading back toward our castle. "Eventually. You still need to get over your "no heir" thing first, of course. But when you do, let me know."

I swaggered through the forest, mentally counting. Guy would get over his stunned shock in three…two…one…

"Robin! You can't just say something like that, then walk away." Guy's boots crunched on the loam as he hurried after me. "We need to talk about this. Robin…"

I gave a hearty laugh and quickened my pace until I was running through the nighttime forest. After a few grumbles, Guy chased after me, occasionally growling my name in a tone that was somewhere between laughter and annoyance.

He would catch me, eventually. He always did, now that I let him. I was his outlaw, and he was my straight-arrow duke. The perfect pair for a legend, even if I did say so myself.

Bonus Extended Epilogue

Here we are at the end.

As Reinhault predicted, Gysborn was inundated with both storms and monsters in the months and years after his death. Yet those same storms and monsters turned into the town's salvation. The storms helped Guy gain respect among the villagers. They might never love him, but they are learning to respect him now that he can show them his true self.

While the monsters proved a tough challenge, the ones we managed to kill provided a source of income for the village. It turns out there is quite the market for exotic meat, poisons, and other items sourced from magical creatures, with the king being our biggest customer.

Yet no matter how many monsters I have killed or will kill, none will be as nightmarish as a certain golden-haired fae with an inviting smile.

As I soon discovered, our outlaw life had been holding back my brothers. John was the next one to get married. He, Will, their wives, and their children are the official foresters, though Guy and I still join a fight or two when we can.

Alan, of course, pursued his dream of becoming a traveling

bard, joined by his wife. His tales of the Hood find a ready audience wherever he travels, though I fear the tales have grown and changed in the telling. The story of the duke's dead wives has separated from the Hood tales, while Maid Marion gained a much larger role, much to Marion's consternation.

Speaking of Marion, he settled down with the village seamstress, and together he and his wife provide the clothing for the village and the castle.

Tuck found his calling in the castle kitchen, and he is all set to take over running the place once our current head cook retires. Tuck lives here in the castle with his wife and children, and I enjoy having a few of my nieces and nephews always around. Sisters-in-law, it turns out, are wonderful. Nothing at all like that fake sister-in-law I'd made up for my cover story.

Munch is the only one who hasn't settled down yet. He bounces between living in the forest with John and Will, joining Alan and his family on their travels, and spending time with Guy and me in the castle. But there is no hurry. He has plenty of time.

As for me and Guy, you don't need to worry. I won't bore you with all the details of how we fell in love. After all, love is like a lot like archery. It starts with a little natural spark, but that spark won't go anywhere until you put in the effort of hard work and time.

When I glance up from writing this, I can see him across the room, making humorous faces at our four-month-old son while changing the baby's dirty swaddling. Our two-year-old daughter clings to Guy's back, begging in that toddler language of hers for her horsey to start tromping around the room again.

Guy's laughter rings above the noise, and it's a beautiful sound I will never get tired of hearing. We are happy, but it is a happiness that came very close to being stolen by the fae.

I write this tale not just to set the record straight, but also to leave a warning to my children, my future grandchildren, and all who happen to read this story.

Beware of fae and their bargains. If it seems too good to be true, then run as far and as fast as you can in the other direction.

I have met good fae. I have even made friends among them.

But those fae come with sincerity and kindness. They give. They don't take. They don't speak slimy words and make slippery bargains.

Learn the lesson of the sadistic fae Reinhault and the duke's murdered wives. Don't forget the cost.

GUYS LEANS OVER MY SHOULDER, now cradling our son in his arms. "You should end it with a line about the importance of love."

I roll my eyes. "I'm not ending this with a clichéd line about love conquering all."

He kisses my cheek. "How about how a legend defeated her greatest enemy and saved the day?"

"Now that sounds like a much better ending." I tip my head and kiss him, as our daughter shrieks at the sight and my pen leaves a large inkstain smeared across the page.

THERE HAVE BEEN many tales told about the Hood. Many of them are nothing but stories.

But the truth of the story is this. I am Robin Hood. I am a legend. And don't you forget it.

Signed,
Lady Robin Hood of Gysborn

Free Book!

Thanks so much for reading *Bluebeard and the Outlaw*! I hope you enjoyed Guy and Robin's romance. If you loved the book, please consider leaving a review on Amazon or Goodreads. Reviews help your fellow readers find books that they will love.

If you would like to see more of Guy, Robin, and especially her youngest brother Munch, their adventures continue in *Forest of Scarlet* (*Court of Midsummer Mayhem Book One*).

If you want to learn about all my upcoming releases, get great book recommendations, and see a behind-the-scenes glimpse into the writing process, sign up for my newsletter and check out my website at www.taragrayce.com.

Did you know that if you sign up for my newsletter, you'll receive lots of free goodies? There are several free Elven Alliance short stories available, along with a standalone fantasy Regency retelling of Beauty and the Beast titled *Torn Curtains*.

You will also receive the free novella *Steal a Swordmaiden's Heart*, which is set in the same world as *Stolen Midsummer Bride* and *Bluebeard and the Outlaw*! This novella is a prequel to *Stolen Midsummer Bride*, and tells the story of how King Theseus of the Court of Knowledge won the hand of Hippolyta, Queen of the Swordmaidens.

Sign up for my newsletter now

Don't Miss the Next Adventure!

FOREST OF SCARLET
(COURT OF MIDSUMMER MAYHEM BOOK ONE)

The fae snatch humans as playthings to torment. The Primrose steals them back.

Vowing that no other family would endure the same fear and pain she felt when her older sister was snatched by the fae, Brigid puts on an empty-headed façade while she rescues humans in the shadowy guise of the Primrose, hero to humans, bane to the fae. Her only regret is that she can't tell the truth to Munch, the young man in the human realm who she's trying very hard not to fall in love with.

Munch has a horrible nickname, an even more terrible full name, and the shadow of his heroic sister and five older brothers to overcome. It's rough being the little brother of the notorious Robin Hood and her merry band. The highlights of his life are the brief visits by Brigid, the messenger girl for the dashing fae hero the Primrose.

When an entire village of humans is snatched by the fae in a single night, Munch jumps at the chance to go to the Fae Realm, pass a message to Brigid and through her to the Primrose, and finally get his chance to be a hero just like all his older siblings.

But the Fae Realm is a dangerous place, especially for a human unbound to a fae or court like Munch. One wrong decision could spell disaster for Munch, Brigid, and the Primrose.

Will this stolen bride's sister and Robin Hood's brother reveal the truth of their hearts before the Fae Realm snatches hope away from them forever?

Loosely inspired by *The Scarlet Pimpernel*, *Forest of Scarlet* is book one in a new fantasy romance / fantasy romantic comedy series of standalones featuring magic libraries, a whimsical and deadly fae realm, and crazy fae hijinks by bestselling author Tara Grayce!

Read on Kindle Today!

Also by Tara Grayce

ELVEN ALLIANCE

Fierce Heart

War Bound

Death Wind

Troll Queen

Pretense

Shield Band

Elf Prince

Peril: Elven Alliance Collected Stories Volume One

Inventor: Elven Alliance Collected Stories Volume Two

COURT OF MIDSUMMER MAYHEM

Stolen Midsummer Bride (Prequel)

Forest of Scarlet

A VILLAIN'S EVER AFTER

Bluebeard and the Outlaw

PRINCESS BY NIGHT

Lost in Averell

Acknowledgments

Thank you to everyone who made this release possible! To my writer friends, especially Molly, Morgan, and Addy for loving Guy and Robin so much! Thanks also to Savannah, Sierra, and the entire Spinster Aunt gang for being so encouraging and helpful. I would not be where I am without you guys! A special thanks to H.S.J. Williams for the lovely artwork of Robin!

A special thanks to my dad and mom, my sisters-in-law Alyssa and Abby, and my brothers. You guys are the best! To Bri for helping me brainstorm Bluebeard and the Outlaw and being so excited about this book! To Paula and Jill for always being excited about my books no matter what I write. To my proofreaders Tom, Mindy, and Deborah, thanks so much for helping to eradicate the typos as much as humanly possible.

A special thanks once again to the entire A Villain's Ever After gang: Camille Peters, Lichelle Slater, Nina Clare, Allison Tebo, Lea Doué, Alesha Adamson, W.R. Gingell, Lucy Tempest, J.M. Stengl, A.G. Marshall, and Sylvia Mercedes. This was such a great experience working with all of you!

Made in the USA
Las Vegas, NV
26 July 2023